MW01199858

HEART
and
SOLE

Miranda Liasson

Entangled Publishing, LLC
2614 South Timberline Road
Suite 109
Fort Collins, CO 80525
Visit our website at www.entangledpublishing.com.

Indulgence is an imprint of Entangled Publishing, LLC.

Edited by Alethea Spiridon Hopson
Cover design by Elizabeth Pelletier

Manufactured in the United States of America

First Edition July 2015

For Mara

Chapter One

Madison Kingston homed in on the tall, elegantly dressed man on the stage with all the desperation of a running back plunging full-force into the end zone. The weight of everything in her life hung in a dreadful, precarious balance, pressing into her chest, making her fight for breath. Reminding her this was the one ball she simply could not drop.

Yet the gorgeous hunk in front of the crowd flashed a nonchalant smile and tossed a carefree wave, as perfectly executed as if he were running for president. He stirred up the women with his darkly handsome, magazine-cover looks, using all his natural-born charisma and carefully-honed charm to reel everyone in. Qualities Maddie was now immune to.

She hoped.

For the sake of saving Kingston Shoes, her family's company, she *had* to be. Ignoring the icicles of fear pricking up and down her spine, she weaved her way through the roomful of high-society guests, closer to the front of the room. In the background, voices murmured and silverware clinked. Taking her seat at one of many elegantly appointed tables, Maddie looked around the high-ceilinged ballroom containing chandeliers dripping with crystals, gaudy red and gold carpet, and well-dressed women wearing gowns made to accentuate cleavage and curves. The smells of finely prepared pan-seared salmon and tender sirloin should have made her mouth water, but her stomach churned in rebellion. Groves of goose bumps riffled over her arms, but not from the cranked-up air conditioning.

They were gathered for the annual *Bachelors with CHOP* event, where ten prominent, unmarried businessmen were auctioned off to benefit the Children's Hospital of Philadelphia. It was a festive evening with dinner, dancing, and, for a handful of lucky bidders, the promise of a weekend with the bachelor of their choice.

The emcee, a silver-haired man in a tux, addressed the guests. "Last but not least, our final bachelor needs no introduction. CEO of his own company, on the boards of many of our city's finest charities, he is a true philanthropist. In addition, he skydives, flies his own plane, and is rumored to own a small island in the Caribbean. Ladies and gentlemen—especially ladies, that is—let's give a big hand to the final bachelor of the Children's Hospital Charity Auction, Mr. Nicholas Holter!"

The high-class crowd bordered on rowdy with all the whoops and hollers. Nick flinched a little amid all the praise, and nervously straightened his tie, actually appearing a little uncomfortable with the attention. Maddie couldn't help but grimace. It had to be an act. Everything about Nick Holter was preplanned and scheduled, including the shining image he'd so carefully crafted.

Was this the same boy she'd adored more than Justin Timberlake, who would impulsively pick her bouquets of wildflowers because he couldn't afford anything else? Who had to borrow a beat-up Chevy Blazer to pick her up for prom? Who'd worked three jobs to earn money for college? She'd loved that boy. But she did not recognize the man.

Nick cleared his throat. "Holter Enterprises is looking to do all we can to help raise money for the new children's cancer ward. We're proud to be part of this town and to have such a great hospital serving our kids. I'm honored to be chosen as one of the lucky guys tonight, and I'll do all I can to ensure that the lovely lady who wins me has a great time. I'm sure it will be a *big* sacrifice on my part."

The crowd laughed, and Nick grinned at the beautiful women waving and fawning over him. Maddie rolled her eyes.

"So come on you all, let's bid high and raise some money for the kids."

You all, he'd said. Not *y'all*. Just a miniscule twinge of rural North Carolina rolled off his tongue, not noticeable to those who didn't know he'd grown up as far off the beaten track as was possible. Maddie was certain he didn't go around bragging — or even admitting — he'd been raised in their small town of Buckleberry Bend. But the little slipup reminded her of the younger, innocent Nick she'd known so well.

"Who knows, Nick?" the emcee joked. "Tonight maybe you'll even find your soul mate. I know half the women here are hoping it will be them."

Maddie let out a disgruntled *tsk*. *Pu-lease*. Auctions like this set women's rights back a full century. Who attended these things, anyway, paying thousands of dollars for the privilege of a weekend in his company like he was some entitled prince?

People like me. Well, at least Maddie didn't want him for herself. It was up to her to step forward and steer Kingston Shoes to success. As soon as she cleared out her office at the graphic design firm she worked for here in Philadelphia, she'd be back home in North Carolina doing exactly that. So what if she had little business experience and a long trail of mistakes that made her entire family's brows arch in skepticism?

She squeezed her eyes closed to shut out her own doubts. She had to leave her past behind. Prove to everyone, including herself, that she could take the reins of this company and make it prosper.

For the hundredth time, Maddie glanced longingly at the bright red exit signs on either side of the stage. It wasn't too late to leave, to cozy-up in her pjs with her DVR'd episodes of *The Bachelor* instead of watching the show live. But staying was the only way she could save the seventy-year-old family business her dad had lovingly run for the past twenty-five years. She could not disappoint him, not after all he'd been through.

Nick chuckled, his handsome face slacking easily into a smile that could break hearts at a single glance. One charming quirk of his gorgeous lips surely got him any woman he wanted.

It had worked on her not so very long ago.

He definitely wasn't looking for his soul mate. That would require having a soul to share, and he'd sold his off, along with his conscience.

Maddie knew better than to take all that male testosterone at face value. She knew what lay beneath the chiseled, determined jaw, the precisely cut head of thick dark hair and that rigid, perfect nose — a ruthless, cunning businessman set on taking over the world at any price.

Starting with her family's company.

Kingston Shoes. Well-engineered, comfortable shoes beloved by generations and fully made in America. Floundering sales brought on by a cheaper foreign market and management problems caused by her dad's recent stroke had sent the company plummeting into a tailspin. And Nick Holter was about to capitalize on it.

The auctioneer began his chatter, starting at a thousand dollars. The previous bachelors had sold for between five and ten thousand, but one had gone as high as twelve. Judging by the crowd's response, Nick would surely go for over ten.

Ten thousand dollars was all she had.

Maddie took a sip of champagne, every muscle tense. This was her last chance, a big, bold gesture of desperation. He'd refused to see her, wouldn't return her calls. His secretary had kicked her to the curb. She needed this time with him, a whole weekend in which he was obligated to hear her out. But maybe even that wouldn't be enough.

She wanted to bring Nick home to his long-forgotten roots. Show him everyone — up close and personal — who would be affected by the company's closing. And pray he still had a small piece of heart left.

All she wanted was a chance to turn the company around — one chance. Al Watson, the CFO, had confessed he'd had to sell off a significant amount of shares for cash flow. Sales were down, very far down. Their brand was suffering. Something needed to be done and fast—before Maddie's father got out of the rehab hospital and learned the company he'd worked for his whole life was going the way of the Twinkie.

But hey, if the Twinkie could come back, so could Kingston Shoes.

Holter Enterprises had bought the stock, giving themselves a forty-two percent stake. At first, Maddie had been in a state of shock. She could not believe Nick had done such a vile thing. To her family, to *her*. Soon he would cajole more stock out of their hands until he controlled the majority. Then he could do a clean sweep of the management, or worse, dissolve Kingston Shoes into a mere pile of dust, another company crumbled in the hands of a venture capitalist giant.

Maddie balled her hands into fists. *No, he would not*. She would *not* permit him to take away their rightful ownership.

She sucked in a deep breath and raised her hand.

"Three thousand dollars."

The auctioneer thrust an arm of acknowledgement in her direction before he scanned the room full of Philly society glitterati and continued his chant. "Three thousand, three thousand five hundred. Do I hear four?"

A few seconds later, the bidding had already soared past four thousand dollars. *Dammit*. Nick Holter was clearly the prime specimen, the man everyone awaited with bated breath, the Brad Pitt of Philadelphia social circles.

A tall blond woman in a slinky floral dress ran the bid up to five thousand. Madison knew her—Gayle Sommers, her sister's boss at the *Philadelphia Inquirer*, a senior editor known for her scathing exposés of political impropriety. And her gorgeous, model-thin body and come-hither eyes promised that her bid for Nick would involve far more than an impulse toward charitable giving. She'd had her sights set on him for quite some time, from what Maddie's sister had told her. Just the type of woman Nick Holter would want— smart, successful, and beautiful.

Maddie lacked the wealth and the cleavage to compete. But she liked to think she made up for that with a determined, animal-like ferocity, honed from years of being The Middle Child.

She's not going to win him. I am.

The only thing that would stand in her way was her drained pocketbook, which was nearing its last dregs. She uncoiled her tightly fisted hand, squeezed it a few times to ensure blood flow. Without hesitation, she raised it high in the air again.

An elegant woman with thick auburn hair in a perfect-ly-coiffed chignon raised a well-manicured hand. Maddie winced. Christie Croft, an heiress and head of a national charity for childhood abuse survivors. Both these women had the potential to outbid her in a heartbeat. Even if by some freak chance she won, she'd be eating a steady diet of macaroni and cheese and ramen noodles for months to come.

The auctioneer's voice droned on. "Six thousand. Do I hear six thousand five hundred…"

Maddie swallowed. This was a bad, bad idea. She struggled, even at this last hour, to think of another plan, but no magical solution appeared. An arm grazed her elbow. Her younger sister, Catherine, sat down next to her. Maddie had stayed in Philadelphia after college, and Cat had followed her here to be closer. "Sorry I'm late. The rain was awful, and I had a hard time getting a cab."

"Seven thousand," the auctioneer yelled.

"Maddie, are you sure you want to do this? Madison!" Catherine tugged urgently on her arm.

Maddie faced her sister. "Yes." Her voice was strangely calm. "I don't have a choice."

Catherine shook her head, her perfectly-in-place blond hair swaying gently. "What you're doing is *not* going to matter. It's too late. Let's leave now while we still can."

"He's ignored all my calls. There's nothing else I can do."

"Nick never used to be like that."

"Well, he is now." Cutthroat. Vicious. A hungry pit bull in the world of business, where meat was meat. "Destroying Kingston Shoes is just one small step in his total takeover of the entire American shoe industry."

"Nick would not destroy us."

The old Nick wouldn't have. But the new Nick...well, that was what he did. Bought up companies and either dismantled them or took them over, depending on their potential for success. Either alternative sucked.

"Maybe you should tell him about Dad."

Madison's stomach lurched. To approach Nick from a position of pity just seemed...wrong. She honestly didn't know if the new Nick would help her or prey on their weakness. "We said we wouldn't let the word out. It will only make our investors panic and put us in an even more precarious spot."

"Maddie, maybe this is about the feud."

The Feud, that awful, mysterious rift between Kingstons and Holters that had torn apart not just their families, but

Nick and her as well.

"That's ancient history. What could it possibly have to do with Nick buying up our company?"

"Maybe he's doing it for his grandfather," Cat said. "You know, like revenge."

"Seven thousand five."

"It doesn't matter why. I have to stop him."

Cat grasped her shoulders and shook, forcing her to make eye contact. "It's too late. For God's sake, at least save your money."

It *couldn't* be too late. Her father couldn't help what had happened. Hell, he didn't even *know* what happened because Maddie and her mom hadn't told him. And if it were up to her, he'd never know.

Just the thought of telling her father that his life's work had dispersed into the wind like so much dandelion fluff sent a tidal wave of determination rolling through her. Some things were more important than money. Like family loyalty. Her grandfather's legacy. Finally making her ailing father proud. She would *not*—could not—allow Nick to take over, no matter what their history.

"You've known each other for years. Can't you figure out a way to connect?"

Maddie made a dismissive gesture with her hand. "I can't even remember when I've seen him last."

A lie. The relentless bids of the auction faded as she remembered with crystal clarity Nick's handsome face hovering above hers, his five-o-clock-stubble scraping deliciously against her cheek, his sinfully full lips lingering in that secret, exquisitely sensitive place between her neck and shoulder. Her breath caught raggedly in her throat as she relived

for the ten-thousandth time that night from a year ago when
they'd both lost all control.

The one and only time in all the years she'd known him.
Fate had always conspired to keep them apart, and always
would. But that night had been unforgettable.

From the second he'd pulled her through the door of his
swanky condo and pressed his lips to hers, she'd turned to
Play Doh in his multitasking hands. Those skilled hands had
circled her waist, pulled her flush against his rock hard body.
His tongue had plied and probed, and she greedily took it
in and gave back all she got, kiss after wet, luscious kiss. She
got lost in the rich spicy scent of his cologne, the wine-laced
taste of his mouth, the thick, silky layers of his hair, even as
her knees threatened to give out and her insides turned to
liquid heat.

If he had just completed four tours in Afghanistan, their
lovemaking couldn't have been more desperate. Ten years of
pent-up desire combusted and exploded in a frantic urgency
that left them both sated and completely shocked.

Okay, that's enough. Madison cleared her suddenly dry
throat and shook her head so she could think. So what if
their one night was fast and furious and out of control and
no man before or since had given her that kind of pleasure?

Well, actually, there hadn't been a *since*. But *he* would
never know that.

The auctioneer's voice became the relentless *clackety-
clack* of a train barreling down the tracks as he headed
into the nine thousand range. Ten thousand dollars was not
enough, she was sure of it now.

She'd already lost all her money and her pride. Those
were nothing compared to the disappointed look in her

father's weary eyes when she told him the truth. *We lost the company, Dad. I'm sorry.*

He'd pat her on the head, tell her she'd done her best and that was all he'd ever asked. But her whole family would all be thinking, *flighty Maddie. Her good intentions gone bad, just like so many times before.*

She turned to her sister. "Catherine, lend me some money."

"No way." Her sister's normally levelheaded tone of voice held a healthy portion of panic.

"He's too popular. It's the only way."

Catherine lowered her voice and gripped Maddie's arm. "Even if you win, it won't make a difference. Bringing him home is like begging. It's time to let it go."

"Please, Catherine. $5,000. I'll pay you back, I swear."

Even as she said the amount, Maddie winced. Her sister was getting married in a year, and she and her insurance actuary fiancé Robert were paying for their own wedding. Putting her in this position was selfish, but right now desperation won over selflessness. "Please."

Precious seconds passed. Practical, sensible Cat scanned Maddie's face, probably seeing a million reasons to run for the hills.

"Ten thousand dollars," the auctioneer announced. The crowd tittered with excitement. Maddie clutched her sister by the shoulders. "Remember John Mayer."

"No. Not that." Cat squeezed her eyes shut, no doubt recalling the time in high school when Maddie had cleaned out her bank account and foregone a new prom dress for ridiculously expensive concert tickets so Cat could take her major crush, who had ultimately stood her up.

"It's not the same." She drilled her gaze at Maddie, who

drilled right back, channeling sister-bond memories of a lifetime.

"For Dad. I have no choice, Cat."

At last Cat released her hand. "Oh, all right. Fine."

Maddie pulled out her chair from the table and hiked up her skirt and her courage. She climbed up, shooting her hand far into the air. Murmurs rose from the people at her table, and she felt the judging stabs of their stares. Who could blame them, since a crazy woman was creating a spectacle in front of a crowd of two hundred? "I pledge $15,000. Plus I'll double that bid with matching corporate funds."

The crowd went silent, corked like an empty champagne bottle.

Maddie's heart slammed into her chest. She barely heard their soft collective gasps. A hot white spotlight showcased her, in the ruby-colored sparkly dress she'd found cheap at a consignment shop, her faux diamond dangling earrings, and the simple shoulder-length hairstyle she'd done herself. Camera bulbs flashed. The voltage of a roomful of nervous energy skyrocketed.

"That's a highly unusual bid, young lady," the emcee finally said. "Frank?" The emcee looked at the auctioneer, who shrugged and for once had nothing to say.

For the first time, Maddie caught Nick's eye, saw the exact moment his body stiffened, his impeccable posture steeling itself even more ramrod straight. His thick brows raised, eyes widening in shock and horror.

"Maddie," he whispered in disbelief. She *heard* him. His mic had picked it up.

The emcee walked over to Nick. "You know this woman?" he asked.

"We're…old friends." He regained his composure in the space of a heartbeat. Lucky him.

She darted her eyes left and right, searching for potential routes of escape. But panic curled icy tentacles around her common sense, paralyzing the urge to flee. The auctioneer whispered something in the emcee's ears. Then the head of the hospital joined the huddle too. Her bid was probably against the rules because it wasn't all in cash. She was so lightheaded, if someone else had bid, she wouldn't have even known.

The auctioneer took the mic from the emcee. "We have a bid of $15,000 cash plus a promise to match it."

Silence.

Please God, Maddie prayed. *I promise I'll visit Great Aunt Ruby as soon as I get into town. I'll double my hours at the food bank. I won't eat chocolate for a year.*

On second thought, at least not chocolate milk.

At last, the auctioneer lowered his arm like a gavel. "Sold! To the young lady in the sparkly dress. Congratulations. You just won yourself a whole weekend with this handsome young fella."

Hands helped her down and music began to play as if she were on some cheesy televised awards show. Cat's expression reflected the horror that must have been evident in her own eyes. "I hope to hell you know what you're doing," she whispered. "Especially since my honeymoon destination just changed from Hawaii to Six Flags."

Maddie walked to the stage to claim her prize, her legs feeling as heavy and clunky as solid lead. Her life savings were drained. Worse, she was in debt. *And* she'd have to spend the next month on the phone soliciting donations from every business colleague she knew. She'd gambled it all on the thin hope that she could convince an unreformed scoundrel not to follow through with the devil's deal.

She wasn't naïve enough to believe she still had the power to influence Nick. But the folks in their town who had worked for their company for years—Nick knew them all too. Surely he wouldn't be unaffected by their plight.

A picture flooded her mind from their one night together. His lithe body stretched out beside her, his head propped casually upon an elbow as his deep chestnut gaze wandered lazily over her body. She'd been spellbound, certain something truly special had been forged between them. But she'd been wrong.

She realized in a weird way she'd just made a wager for Nick Holter's humanity. She'd bet everything on it, even when she already knew he'd bartered it away long ago.

Chapter Two

Nick Holter shaded his eyes from the bright spotlights as he watched a familiar figure part the crowd. A combination of anticipation and dread filled him. *Madison Kingston*. The woman from his past who just wouldn't disappear, out of his mind or out of his life. The very *last* woman he'd ever expected to bid for him at a charity auction.

An inaudible curse escaped his lips. He hated that his heart stuttered wildly as she approached. Even worse, his first rampant thought had been that she'd come here for *him*, found a way for them to be together.

No way. She had to be angry. He hadn't returned her calls. And he couldn't help her, no matter how much a very large part of him was tempted to. It was better to stay away.

So much for that plan.

Because here she was, wearing a fire-hydrant-red dress that clung to every curve, her hips sashaying gently as she worked her way to the stage. Wavy hair the color of rich bold coffee grazed her shoulders—much longer than when he'd seen her last. Her devil-may-care smile caressed the crowd, like she kept a secret they wished they'd be privy to, and she nodded and laughed as if she didn't have a care in the world.

Beautiful. Sleek. Professional. Not the uncoordinated eight-year-old who constantly scraped her knobby knees falling off her sparkly purple Huffy bike with the red, white, and blue streamers.

He sucked in a sharp breath. He hadn't hallucinated.

Madison locked gazes with him, and his stomach plummeted, a knotted ball of dread. It was her, all right, the hometown girl he'd left behind, disguised as a siren with glossy red lips that matched her sexy, clingy dress. She was even more beautiful than in his fantasies. He still dreamed of those curves under him and over him, those sweet soft lips caressing him everywhere, murmuring bedroom phrases or just releasing little gasps of pleasure as he—

No. They'd gone there once and it was a big mistake. The worst.

They'd never had a chance, not after all the bad blood that still flowed between Kingstons and Holters, creating a river of bitterness that swept away all the good their families had once forged together.

He'd chosen loyalty to his grandfather who had raised him. He'd had no choice.

Besides, a woman like Maddie expected things he couldn't give. Things he didn't know *how* to give. He'd once lost everything in the flash of a second—his parents, his baby sister—and a wound like that stayed with a man. And yet something niggled in the back of Nick's brain: his conscience. He was an expert in keeping business and emotion separate, compartmentalized. But right now the boxes were threatening to burst open and mix it all up.

Madison hitched up her sparkly dress a little so she could climb the stairs to the stage. Long, slender legs in red sky-high heels peeked out. A security guard moved to help her up, but Nick interceded and held out his own hand. Hers was warm and soft and small, easily engulfed by his large one. The simple act of touching her made his pulse gallop. Startled sapphire eyes leapt up at him as if it disarmed her too. Seeing her up close—the rich jewel tones of her eyes, those full, kissable lips, and the smooth swells of her breasts under her form-fitting gown—made him ache to touch more intimate parts of her as he had so thoroughly a year ago.

The crowd whooped and hollered around them, but he barely noticed. "Hello, Madison." He tried to make his voice sound calm and unaffected, but even to him it sounded tinged with nerves.

She nodded. "Nick." Her gaze met his, now cool and precise as a knife's edge. But as he escorted her to the stage, her arm under his hand was trembling. Had he imagined that quick flash in her aqua blue eyes of expectation, pleasure, maybe even hope?

It caught him off guard, but he didn't flounder. He could handle this in front of the crowd. He was an expert at people pleasing. The king of masks. She would never see his vulnerabilities. He flashed her his most winning smile.

"Congratulations. You've got me for an entire weekend."

"A *long* weekend, I hope." A trace of a smile turned up the corner of her full, lush mouth.

She was up to something, he was certain. But he wanted to disarm her. So he slid his hand up her bare back as they walked together toward the emcee. "The longer the better," he said.

His plan backfired. Her skin was soft as a down feather, and she smelled heavenly—some scent that was spicy and floral but not cloying. Fresh and simple and far removed from his world full of empty lavishness. Just like her.

It took him back immediately to that night a year ago. They'd had dinner, drinks. Then gone back to his place, a penthouse apartment where he often stayed when business took him to Atlanta. French doors opened to a balcony surrounded by the velvet night. Thousands of lights twinkled beyond the manicured bougainvillea, the city showing off its best just for them.

The expansive ballroom suddenly felt hot and stuffy. Nick thrust a finger under his collar and craned his neck to loosen it. He had to get a grip. *It was only sex.* It was unlike him to invest so much time reliving a memory, a dream that could never be.

The emcee tilted his microphone toward Maddie. "How do you feel, Ms. Kingston, about winning your bachelor?"

Madison smiled brightly, the picture of poise and grace. "I'm thrilled to contribute to such a great cause. Children's Hospital will always be near and dear to my heart." She clutched her chest, a gesture of sincerity he knew was real. Her twin nephews had been born prematurely in Philly and had spent two long months there.

"But tell us why you're so eager to win Mr. Holter?"

She tossed a wide smile in Nick's direction. "Who wouldn't be eager for such a handsome hunk?"

She's playing you, Nick. Be careful. His mind understood, but his body was nothing but a traitor.

"My plan is to take Nicky back to our hometown in North Carolina for a big family weekend. And I actually have a proposition for him." She turned from the microphone, looked directly at him.

A provocative *ooooh* shot up from the crowd. They were loving every minute. He shot her a cautionary glare, but she paid no heed.

The emcee interjected. "Wait a minute. You two grew up together?"

"We did. And it's been far too long since he's been back." She orchestrated a suggestive wink that indicated all the rehearsing she'd done senior year to play the part of Blanche DuBois in *A Streetcar Named Desire* had really paid off. "I hope this isn't too much to ask, but since I did offer to match my donation with corporate funds, I was wondering if I can get Nick to agree to just two more days—the long Fourth of July weekend."

No way. It was hard to smile through such a rigidly clenched jaw, but somehow Nick struggled through it.

"I know what you're thinking," she said. "You're a busy guy and don't take much time off. But I can guarantee that everyone in Buckleberry Bend wants to see how their hometown son made good. And you can't miss the Berry Festival."

He nearly rolled his eyes. A measly extra fifteen grand that would take her months to raise was not worth an extra two days of his time in Podunkville.

The emcee reiterated the deal. "Another fifteen thousand dollars in matching funds if Nick makes it a long weekend to reconnect in his hometown—and do it with this beautiful woman? What do you say, Nick?"

The crowd cheered. They clearly liked her. He had to be

careful.

"I want to thank Ms. Kingston for her generous gift to the hospital. I must say I'm flattered. And pleased to make the trip back home. But I'd like to insist on matching Ms. Kingston's donation myself."

And skip the extra two days. Maybe he could pay her off and skip the whole thing entirely.

"That's very generous of you, Nick," the emcee said. "But I have to ask, where the heck is Buckleberry Bend, anyway?"

Madison explained the nestled-in-the-foothills location as Nick tried not to wince.

The emcee nudged them together so their shoulders touched. "Before we close our event for the evening, how about a kiss to cap off the night?"

"Gladly." Nick hammed for the crowd, rubbing his hands together in anticipation. Up close, he could see the cold, sharp intelligence in her eyes. But as he inched closer, something else appeared—a rare softening. Maybe a flicker of hurt. It lasted only an instant before he grasped her shoulders and pulled her close to plant a decadent, full-mouthed kiss on those rosy, glistening lips.

It started out as a kiss of control, of power, but damn if she didn't get to him. She wrapped her slender hand around his neck and pressed herself to him, pushing her tongue inside his mouth. The heat of her sweet body nearly melted him. Their tongues jousted for dominance, a sensuous battle of wills that left him out of breath and wanting.

Then suddenly she broke away.

"What are you up to, Madison?" he whispered into her ear.

Her only response was a cat-got-your-tongue smile.

They held hands for the crowd, waved, and made their exit off the curtained stage.

He trailed after her, following the glint of her dress into the backstage shadows, but the director of the auction, Grace McLaughlin, waylaid him with a big hug.

"Nick, we can't thank you enough for participating. Thirty thousand dollars for the hospital is nothing to sneeze at. And she's adorable. You're going to the after party, aren't you?"

"Grace, glad to do what I can." He didn't want to attend the after party, but he was obligated. There would be interviews and photo ops, all of it excellent publicity for the auction and the hospital.

He left Grace's side and walked through the backstage area, looking everywhere for Madison. He had a million questions and needed to get to the bottom of this.

But she was gone.

Chapter Three

On Monday morning, Maddie was on the phone in her office when Nick leaned his large-shouldered frame across her desk, carefully moving her stiletto shoe stapler out of the way. Her sketchbook filled with shoe designs lay millimeters from his hand. As she instinctively buried it under a stack of papers, their fingers brushed, sending an unwanted frisson of energy zipping up her arm.

She stiffened, all her defenses snapping into place. Just because he strode in looking more mouthwatering than her mother's famous peach pie, his graphic tie and dress shirt straining against taut, hard muscles *and* smelling like Italian cologne, did *not* mean she was intimidated.

Melting inside and short of breath, definitely, but intimidated, *no*.

She rolled her eyes to show she wasn't, moved her stapler out of his reach, and continued her business call.

He waited about a second after she hung up before he

spoke. "Why wouldn't you meet me in my room to talk after the party? Didn't you get my note?" His tone bespoke a man unused to being stood up.

"I never engage the enemy on his own turf. Besides, the last time I met you in your room, our 'talk' didn't go so well."

He snorted. Their "talk" last year had lasted all of sixty seconds before their clothes were off, and they were engaging in very *un*-businesslike forms of communication. She still remembered how, in the dark bedroom, the outside lights had played across the strong, stubborn planes of Nick's face, the sculpted hills and hollows of his perfectly formed chest. He'd looked at her tenderly, lifted a lock of her hair, and flashed the sweetest smile. As if their lovemaking had allowed him, for an all-too-brief flash of time, to drop that heavily guarded wall he kept shuttered fast around him.

Remorse pricked her. She'd allowed herself to dream big after that night, and it still really hurt. She didn't want him to think the auction had anything whatsoever to do with *them*. Too bad he was Enemy Number One, no matter how tempting the package. And she couldn't ever forget it.

Nick slowly lowered his tall frame into one of the leather chairs across from her desk and stretched out his long legs, muscles molding against form-fitting, freshly creased pants that probably cost more than her monthly rent.

She resisted the urge to fan herself. Did she say *tempting package*? That would be correct. She glanced at her phone to fight the distraction. "Don't get too comfortable. I have an appointment in ten minutes."

"That should be more than enough time to sort this through. I want the truth, Madison. All of it."

She swiveled around in her chair. "I want you to come

home and see my family. And our town. That's the whole truth."

And then I want you to realize this whole scheme is wrong, dump your shares, and let me take over as CEO. Easy peasy.

"You want me to sell my investment in your company, and I won't do it."

His eyes scanned the painted wood sign that hung behind her desk. It read *Integrity. Honesty. Hard Work.* Underneath, in smaller lettering, it read *Kingston Shoes. Family Owned Since 1944.*

"Stop it," she said.

"Stop what?" he asked innocently.

"Stop judging our company."

"I find it ironic you think you stand for all those things, but you don't."

"You don't know what I stand for."

"Maybe not, but my grandfather does."

She sighed. "Why does every discussion we have come back to this?"

"Because my grandfather helped build your company with his integrity, honesty, and hard work, and all he got was screwed."

"He walked away was the story I heard. And the company was too young at the time to have much return on investments."

Nick snorted. "Without my grandfather's engineering genius, your shoes would never have taken off in the first place."

"Is that why you bought up shares? Because you're out for revenge?"

"No." He stood and tapped his index finger down on the surface of her cluttered desk to underscore his point. "I'm out for *justice*." He paused to see the effect of his words, but she purposely faced him unflinching. "Besides, you need to add another word to your motto."

She crossed her arms defiantly.

"*Modernization*. Your company is out of date."

Maddie stood so fast the wheels on her chair clattered against the plastic carpet guard beneath. She heaved deep breaths in and out to remain calm.

It didn't work.

"Our orthopedic line got a top rating from *Consumer Reports* for quality and engineering."

"They're old lady shoes. The real shoe-buying demographic won't touch them."

She made a mental note not to allow Nick a glimpse of her own shoes, which happened to be passion pink four-inch peek-toe pumps with ruffle embellishments that were definitely *not* from the Kingston collections.

"So they're practical. We're not targeting the uber-stylish-designer crowd." But that would change once she was in charge. If she could get her designs noticed. Like in the national Bergdorf design competition she was thinking about entering.

"You're not targeting *any* market. That's the problem. You're wasting opportunities by putting forth a bland product."

Maddie suddenly realized both her hands were clamped into fists. He was the most irritating, cutthroat, opportunistic know-it-all she'd ever met and she wanted to tell him so, only she knew her father would disapprove. He'd taught her and her siblings to treat people civilly, with a smile, even if they made you mad as hell. "Treat 'em like kings and queens, because they're our bread and butter," he'd admonished when they were teenagers, working in the original store on Main Street.

Her heart twisted. Henry Kingston was old school all the way. A proud man who didn't let on to any of them that the company was in trouble even before he'd had the stroke that took away his speech and ability to walk.

But if Nick knew her dad was sick he'd shut them down—or take over—in less than a heartbeat. She'd never get the chance to bring the company back to its feet. "Why do you care about our products if you're going to dissolve the company anyway?"

"I'm only stating facts. The company is in a tailspin. My job is deciding which companies to save and which to let go, and based on every indicator, it's too late."

He sat in his chair, relaxed, confident and so damn smug she wanted to wrinkle his shirt. Mess up his hair. Skew his tie. Anything to see if he was really human under all that arrogance.

"The bottom line is that you're capitalizing on our bad fortune. How could you take away our livelihood?" She bit her lip. She sounded desperate. Angry. When she should be calm, logical, and unaffected.

"My grandfather was never able to achieve a dream he still wants. I have the opportunity to give that to him. I'm sorry, Maddie." For a second, he looked genuinely contrite. His large brown eyes filled with softness, like he truly did regret being a scumbag. But then they went hard. "Business is business."

She lowered herself back into her chair. "No, Nick, business is *never* just business. Especially in this case."

"I can't help what happened between our grandfathers. But I can help make it right."

"Do you really think that taking over the company on behalf of your grandfather is going to avenge a fifty-year-old feud?" It certainly wouldn't end it. She shuddered as she imagined the flash of horror on her family's faces if Kingston Shoes were ever owned by Holters.

"Maybe not." He paused. "Look at it this way. If it's not me, it's going to be somebody else. Your company is sinking faster than the Titanic."

His grandfather was seventy-two, just like her grandmother. What on earth was he going to do with their company?

Nick's gaze flitted around the room. Half-packed boxes lay strewn on the floor, and one of the bookshelves was empty. Maddie shifted in her chair, a vain attempt to distract him from all the evidence of her moving.

"You're leaving?"

She stiffened. "My father needs help. I believe I can help him turn things around."

A frown cast a shadow on his strong features. "I always thought you didn't want anything to do with the business."

She hadn't. She was an artist at heart, much to her dad's chagrin. A few years ago, after graduating from the Art Institute of Philadelphia with her graphic design degree, her parents had loaned her money for a website design startup that had failed disastrously. But she finally landed a decent job, managing a group of graphic designers who created ads for different online shoe companies.

And in her spare time, she drew shoes. Stilettos, pumps,

platforms, booties, sandals…velvet, satin, bead, and embroidery embellishments…stuff far, far away from the practical leather 'n' laces she'd been surrounded by her entire life. A useless skill as far as her dad was concerned, who had begged her to get a business degree so she could take over the company books. But now her father needed her, and she wouldn't let him down. She *couldn't*.

"I changed my mind."

This was the impasse. The old family feud that had no end. No one even knew what it was about anymore.

"Look, I didn't come here to dredge up the past." Nick turned and stretched out one leg so he could pull a piece of paper out of his pocket, which he tossed blithely across the desk.

It was a check for $30,000 made out to Children's Hospital.

Maddie raised her brow, resisted the urge to tear the flimsy sheet to shreds and rant. *Be calm. Be rational. Let him explain.* "What's this for?"

She may have been trained in graphic design, but she could add. Her bid plus her promise. Thirty-K. Enough to forget her whole stupid plan and let him off scot-free.

"Take it, and we can pretend last night never happened. You'll be off the hook to cough up all that money I know you don't have."

Bright, angry fireworks burst in front of her eyes, obscuring her vision. Oh, she'd take it all right…and shove it right up his elegant, conceited ass.

Even worse, his words brought back another night, a year ago, and she wondered if he wished *that* night had never happened either.

"What you're really saying is *you're* off the hook," she

said.

"Hardly."

She crossed her arms in a not-so-fast move. "The rules state you have to spend the weekend with me. The *long* weekend."

A wry, cocky smile washed across his face. "If you want me that bad, we can spend a weekend wherever you want, sweetheart."

"You arrogant, cocky bastard."

She walked around her desk, no longer caring if he noticed her impractical shoes, until they were face to face. "I do *not* want you sexually, but you are going to fulfill the terms of the agreement. You can't make up your own rules."

His gaze drifted slowly down her body, and she suppressed a shiver. She detected a glimmer of amusement in the depths of his caramel-colored eyes. He *knew* she wanted him, and he reveled in her weakness. "It's a charity auction—there are no technical 'rules.'" He drew quotation marks in the air.

"We'll see about that." Maddie picked up her cell phone from the desk and punched in a number.

Nick's brows shot up in concern. "What are you doing?"

"Calling my sister."

"Which one?"

"Not Liz—she's still overseas doing doctor stuff." He moved to snatch the phone from her hand but she backed up and began talking. "Hi, Cat. Nick's in my office. He wants to pay me off to drop the auction agreement."

"So let him," her sister said.

Maddie pretended not to hear. "I want to instruct him about the backlash that would create."

"Backlash? Money talks. As long as he pays, there's no backlash."

Maddie held the phone against her shoulder. "Catherine says she'll make sure it gets written up in her column that you reneged. You'll have to answer to the entire city. Plus, they want to do a follow-up article after our 'date.'" This time *she* made the air quotes. "Your reputation as a nice guy is at stake. And I know how much you care about what other people think."

She walked around him. He stood arrow-straight and tall, shoulders back, posture perfect. But a tiny vein at his temple pulsed. His square jaw clenched hard, and so did his fist. Mr. Cool-as-a-Cucumber was sweating.

And that was a beautiful thing.

"The agenda is set." She ticked off events on her fingers as she paced back and forth in front of her desk. "First, we'll see my family." Well, minus her father, but maybe she could tell him her dad was gone on business. "Then we'll attend the Berry Festival. And then there's Gran's seventy-second birthday. Mom's already insisted you stay with us."

"That's very kind. But I'll stay at the B and B, thanks."

"My parents have never held your genes against you, Nick." Plus, there was no way her mother was going to allow that. She could bet her firstborn—if she ever had one—on it. But now his eye was twitching, and she didn't want to push her luck.

"I just don't want to make anyone uncomfortable."

"Then don't do this to us."

"I bought shares, that's all. Shares that were up for sale because you all are desperate." His voice was soft, almost soothing. "The company has failed all by itself. It needs a miracle to save it, and I'm sorry, but I'm fresh out of those. This trip is going to be a waste of time for both of us."

Maddie felt the shock of his touch on her arm. Even now, waves of heat spread through her body. *Damn him anyway.* She tried to pull out of his reach, but his hold was steel, and his hard, calculating gaze bored into hers. He was not a man who lost his battles.

She shook her head like he was a hopeless case, but deep down, Maddie wondered if it was really herself she was chiding.

Nick's dark, sensual eyes bore into hers. "You've spent money you can't afford and now you're leaving your job for a lost cause. Give it up, Maddie. I'm going to dissemble or restructure whether I share a piece of birthday cake with your grandmother or not."

She swallowed hard. Could he do either with just over a forty percent stake? She didn't understand business that well, but Nick was a very powerful man. She was certain he could create a hell of a lot of havoc.

Was the old Nick in there somewhere? The one who snuck a red rose onto her pillow for her sixteenth birthday. Who got caught in a downpour walking home with her from the library, when they stopped in Crenshaw's barn to get warm and ended up making out and late for dinner. All the sneaking around they'd done for most of senior year. All the pain of losing a love she once thought was perfect.

Before she could wax too sentimental, she made herself remember that Nick had broken up with her right after prom senior year. Told her he was moving on to other things. He'd never admit it, but she knew he'd overheard her grandmother calling him trailer trash. Maddie had pleaded and begged, told him it didn't matter to her what anyone said, but he'd wasted no time dating her nemesis, a gorgeous bombshell who lived to make her miserable. Then he left the simple life they'd led in their hometown for everything bigger and better. And left her behind without a glance back.

The old Nick was gone.

"You're right." She stepped out of his reach and gave the boy she once loved a pensive look. "Visiting our company and eating cake with my gran and seeing everyone you left behind years ago is not going to change your mind. But it's going to give me something you'll never understand."

"What's that?"

"Closure. I want you to face my family and own up to your decisions."

She saw the struggle in his eyes as they narrowed down on her. Concession was a real bitch. "All right. You win. But I have conditions." He ticked them off on his elegant fingers. "I don't stay at your house. I'll tell your family about the deal on my own terms. I'm not going to endure interrogation and conviction all weekend. Lastly, I don't tour the company. There's no need. I'll see it when it's mine."

Maddie tapped the tips of her nails against the glass surface of her desk and almost smiled. He'd always had a need for control, for order. As a child who lost his parents young and was raised by the grandfather who'd been ousted from the business, Nick had grown up with more than his share of disorder.

There was no point in arguing about details now. She'd have to work them out later, once she had him back in Buckleberry. "I'll pick you up Wednesday at five p.m." She straightened papers in hopes he would take the hint and leave.

"Wait. We're not flying?"

"I usually drive." In reality, she was broke. She'd be lucky to afford the gas.

"I'll have my pilot fly us."

She was not going to allow him to control this situation. First it would be his private plane, then it would be his entourage of minions to seal the deal. "I—I'm afraid to fly." Maddie bit the insides of her cheeks to stop from saying more.

"You never used to be." A suspicious frown creased his perfect forehead.

"It—um—happened recently. A near-death experience. Over the Atlantic." She bit down hard, the metallic taste of blood bitter in her mouth.

A frown creased his perfect forehead. "I am *not* driving eight and a half hours with you."

"That's why we're leaving Wednesday afternoon after work. So we still have plenty of time once we get home."

"Wait a minute," he said. "We agreed on four days. That would mean we leave Thursday."

"Technically not, because you'll be back by five on Sunday. Thus four days starts Wednesday afternoon."

"Fine," he growled, pulling a sticky note off a pad on her desk to scribble down his address.

"I remember where you live," she whispered.

As he handed her the note, their fingers touched. Warm, solid. Their gazes locked, his as steely and uncompromising as their conversation. Maddie fought the impulse to grab his hands, shake them, pull him to her. *Stop this craziness*, every fiber in her wanted to cry out. *We can be bigger than this*.

Better than this.

"I know you do." His voice was soft. For just a second, he sounded like the old Nick. They stood there, each holding on to the note, their hands still touching, the weight of many unsaid words cluttering the space between them.

What if they could put an end to this right now? Say the rift had to end. Work to mend instead of widen it. She opened her mouth to speak. All it would take was one of them to start.

Nick abruptly pulled his hand away. "Good-bye, Maddie. See you tomorrow." Then he turned and walked his gorgeously tight butt out of her office, not bothering to glance back.

Who was she kidding? While she remembered a sweet, innocent Nick from long ago, he had morphed into a hard-chiseled shark who conducted his business without regard for hardship.

She thought she'd cracked through his hard outer shell a year ago, but she was wrong. It was impermeable to emotion.

He was going to be the same major pain in the ass as always. If she didn't find some way to chip through, this trip wouldn't change a thing. It would just make her more broke and more unable to help her family.

Maddie pulled out her buried sketchbook and thumbed through the pages of charcoaled drawings. She had so many ideas, but not a clue how to make an actual shoe. Nick was right. No one at Kingston Shoes would agree to try her out-of-the-box designs.

"By the way," Nick said, suddenly appearing in the doorway. She startled and slammed the notebook closed. How long had he been standing there?

"Nice shoes, but not exactly consistent with the current Kingston inventory."

Her face flooded with heat. Panic muted her voice as she struggled for a reply, not wanting to hand him a weapon to use against her. It took a second to realize he was not staring at her precious designs, but at her shoes.

Maddie contemplated tossing one at him to wipe the patronizing grin off his too-handsome face, but he'd vanished before she could pull it off her foot. It was going to be a very long weekend.

Chapter Four

Maddie exited the coffee shop they'd stopped at not even five minutes into their trip, which irked Nick to no end. He pulled up his black Lexus coupe so she wouldn't get wet, watching the wipers glide efficiently back and forth in front of him. At least he'd insisted on taking his car instead of the old bucket of bolts she'd called Bessie, a pink PT Cruiser that had seen better days.

And he'd insisted on driving. Rain always made him edgy, reminded him of that stormy night long ago that had caused the accident that claimed his parents and baby sister and changed his life forever. It was better for him to stay in control rather than worry, and for him that meant taking the wheel.

His irritation drained as he saw her, armed with caffeine and full of eager anticipation. She wore a Phillies cap with her hair pulled back in a ponytail, yoga pants, and a T-shirt. How could she look so fresh and simple—nothing like the tempting seductress from the auction—yet still set his blood to boiling?

A surge of heat flared in his abdomen from viewing the fine curves of her nicely rounded derriere in those skin-tight pants, curves that turned his thoughts to cupping that sweet behind, running his hands along those smooth calves, and ending their road trip in the penthouse suite at a five-star downtown hotel.

But it was the memories of that same smiling, expectant girl that really pummeled him. She'd always approached any trip, no matter how small, as an adventure, and her enthusiasm had been contagious. He snorted. *Dumb kids.* He opened the passenger door and pushed those thoughts from his mind. All he wanted was to survive the next couple of days and forget about the Maddie chapter in his life.

"I got you a black coffee. Is that how you take it?"

"Thanks," he mumbled.

"Plain. Black. Nothing added." She peeked under his lid, and the rich, earthy smell of good strong coffee infiltrated the car.

He steered the car into the throng of late afternoon rush-hour traffic exiting the city. "What's wrong with that? What'd you order, a non-fat-girlie-skim-no-whip-something or other?"

"Not even close." She shook her drink and ice cubes rattled against the plastic cup. "This is an iced mocha with whip. *Lots* of whip."

"My life is simpler."

"Your life is black and white. Either, or."

Traffic crawled. The wipers *chink-chinked.* The smell of summer rain was thick in the air. Nick needed to focus on getting them out of here, not on trading insults.

"Could we call a truce, please?"

Out of the corner of his eye, he saw her wary look. She wasn't wearing an ounce of makeup, but her skin was creamy smooth. She looked young and innocent, and it reminded him of wonderful days when he thought she was the most beautiful girl he'd ever seen.

She still was.

He had to remind himself that he was the one who'd ended it between them…twice. Left that small town behind so he could become something big. Something better. What could a poor kid from the rangy side of town offer the daughter of one of the most well-to-do families, anyway?

Nick tapped his fingers against the steering wheel. "Maybe we need rules," he said.

She groaned. "What is it with you and your rules?"

"They keep me organized. On track." And kept his mind off her.

"In Black and White World."

"First rule, no insults."

"That might be impossible." Her lips closed carefully around the straw. Sweat broke out on his forehead. How could she make sipping on a straw erotic?

"Look, I agreed to this hokey trip. The least you could do is be decent about it."

She folded her arms and set her chin to a defiant tilt. "Fine."

"Rule two. We don't discuss business. It's a sore point, so we should avoid it. And three, let's try to be pleasant."

He saw her jaw twitch. He could tell she was gnawing the insides of her cheeks again. "Okay," she said. Her straw made a noise as she hit the bottom of her drink, sucking up every last drop.

"That was fast."

"It's too good to drink it slow."

"You're not a savor-it-slowly type of person?"

"With coffee drinks, no. But with people and friends and fun activities, I would say I very much am. How about you?"

He didn't know how to answer that. His life seemed to be a speeding train headed as fast as possible toward his goal of being successful. No, more than successful. The Best.

Maybe it had a lot to do with his grandfather who never achieved his dream of becoming a first-class shoe designer. Who'd given up going to New York City after Nick's parents died and he'd taken on the responsibility of raising Nick.

At least Nick had made something of his life, far away from Buckleberry Bend. Gramps wouldn't take the new BMW he'd sent and had made him retract the offer he'd made on a brand new luxury condo outside of town. But now Nick finally held the trump card that would pay back his grandfather for all the sacrifices he'd made.

He was going to give Gramps the chance he'd always wanted, his dream to get his shoe designs in front of big shots. And Nick was going to do it with the very company that had taken that dream away so long ago.

He didn't want to hurt Madison or her family, but if he didn't buy their company, someone else would. That was life. Sometimes you had to do painful things regardless of the consequences.

He felt her quietly assessing him, her gaze flicking disapprovingly from his high-end polo to his Italian leather shoes that to her surely bespoke luxury and money. To her, he was the epitome of a crass billionaire.

"Are you sure you want to waste your time and mine following through with this?" he asked.

She sat up straight. "I've been reading some of the company documents. You own forty-two percent of the company as of last month when my Uncle Al sold his shares. So you are *not* a majority owner."

Actually, he was. One of his companies had bought up shares several years ago under the name Viper, Incorporated. A different public face than Holter Capital but the same person in charge. *Himself.*

Maddie continued. "I have ideas to save the company. To turn it around, make it bigger and better than before."

Startlingly blue eyes looked straight into him. She was so…hopeful. Even now, he still hated to burst the bubble of her undying optimism, even though he held no such naïve beliefs himself.

Tell her. Tell her now that you already own the majority of the company. He could have said it from the get-go and made this entire trip unnecessary, but he didn't need the backlash that would come his way in the press. Besides, it would be worth it to check out the company that would soon be his. Then he'd find a way to break it to her gently that Holter ownership of Kingston Family Shoes was already a done deal.

Somehow, the triumphant emotions he thought he'd feel over finally bringing justice to his grandfather didn't feel so amazing with Maddie sitting right next to him. "There's still time to go back. I'll be honest with you. Success in this case is as rare as a sunny day in Cleveland."

A spark of defiance lit up her eyes. "When a sunny day

comes, I'm sure the people up there on Lake Erie really appreciate it."

"I think you're foolish, but—"

"You just broke rule one," Maddie said. Actually, they were talking business *and* it was unpleasant. Strikes two and three.

"I did," Nick said. "Sorry about that."

"It's all right." She covered a sudden yawn with the back of her hand.

The rain finally began to slow, and the traffic pick up from its crawl as he headed west on I-76, the first of many highway miles that would eventually lead them to Buckleberry Bend.

Soon the soft sound of Maddie's breathing assured him she was asleep, despite just sucking down a drink that contained two shots of espresso. Bantering back and forth with her had been strangely fun. She'd always had a wicked sense of humor whereas he'd tended to be overly serious. He was certain she had a gaggle of friends—always had.

A profound sense of sadness permeated deep inside of him like a chill on a bitter winter day. He had friends, all right—mostly hangers-on impressed by his wealth and the perks that offered them. Besides his long-time business partner, Preston Guthrie, who else did he really trust? Who did he hang out with to just…hang out? Flying to Vail to ski, to New York to catch a show, to Vegas to wine and dine his latest conquest—his life was filled with beautiful women, spontaneity, and lots of adventure. Yet as he drove along listening to the rhythm of the wipers and Maddie's quiet breathing as she slept, none of it seemed genuine or real.

"Nick?" His traveling companion had nestled down in her seat, kicked off her tennis shoes and stuck her feet on the dashboard. Her toes were painted a deep, sparkly blue. Whimsical. Another stark contrast from the cool and collected businesswoman from the other day.

Her eyes were drifting closed again, so he spoke softly. "What is it?"

"Let me know when you want me to drive. I'm ready anytime."

Right.

"Oh, and Nick?"

"Yes, Madison."

"Life might be more fun if you broke a couple rules along the way."

He wouldn't know. Rules had saved him. Given him order and purpose. He had played by them for so long, he had no clue what it was like not to.

Chapter Five

They switched drivers somewhere in Virginia, although Maddie had to practically pry Nick's hands off the wheel to get him to surrender it. Why he'd been so insistent, she had no idea, but when he started to bounce his left knee and hum Beatles music loudly and out of tune to stay awake, there was no way she was going to let him drive eight hours straight.

Ahead, open highway rolled and stretched surrounded by green, tree-covered mountains. It was almost as interesting as the six-foot-plus, luscious-man-scenery dozing beside her.

Sleep did something to a man. Especially *this* man, and whatever that was, she felt it clear down to her toes. Softened the edges, released the tension that normally held his jaw and brow taut. Watching his face assume a peaceful expression was mesmerizing…and dangerous.

A sign should read *Wolf-in-sheep's-clothing. Danger!*

As if sensing her perusal, Nick startled and bolted

upright in his seat. "Where are we?"

"Whoa there." She reached out to place her hand on his arm. Muscles tensed and flexed beneath her touch. The man was seriously on edge. It surprised Maddie how he could appear so calm on the outside, yet his insides were wound tight as a rubber band ready to snap.

She glanced at her dashboard GPS and tried to sound cheery. "We'll be there in only five more hours."

He sighed.

"We don't need to make small talk. If you'd like, we could invent more rules."

He burst out laughing. A low, spontaneous rumble. It sort of jarred her. The fact that she'd caused it made her feel strangely pleased.

"How about we stop for a burger instead?" he asked.

The idea of sinking her teeth into a warm juicy burger made her stomach tremble with anticipation. She'd been eating an awful lot of peanut butter after tossing so much of her own money at the company this past year.

She paused as an old memory surfaced. "Remember the picnic we took to Spiders' Cove that one summer?"

Nick crossed his arms like maybe he was trying to hold the memories back, but cracked a smile. "With a name like that, we should've known better."

Madison waved her hand dismissively in the air. "Oh, we were young and adventurous. Hey, didn't you need antibiotics for those spider bites on your butt?"

"Ten days' worth."

"All that sneaking around wasn't worth it, huh?" She shouldn't have said that. She didn't need reassurance or proof that he'd once loved her.

He paused so long she thought he wasn't going to answer. "It was worth it."

Darned if her stupid heart didn't do a flip-flop. Maddie's face flamed with fire, and she forced herself to concentrate on driving.

"Once my grandfather and your grandmother got wind of us dating, they did everything imaginable to stop us." He stared out the window, deep in thought.

"But we didn't listen, did we?"

They fell into silence. The ghost of old memories cast a pall Maddie was eager to erase. But this time she couldn't find a ready quip to shrug it off.

He seemed to sense the change in her mood. "Life's a lot different than it was then."

He wasn't kidding. She thought of her job, her dad, the impossible task ahead of her at the end of this road trip. Definitely not the carefree youth she'd remembered.

"We were both idealistic," Nick said. "Believed we could conquer the world. We didn't understand that life has a way of changing your dreams."

"I still believe in dreams."

"What might those be?"

Well, number one on her dream list was to enter her sexiest, sleekest, most glittery shoe design in Bergdorf's national *Get Your Shoe in the Door* competition. Grand Prize was a one-year contract to appear in Bergdorf's store—and a whole lot of attention. Just what Kingston Shoes needed.

Maddie knew she was really, really good at drawing shoes. Translating that into 3-D was another story. But she wasn't about to tell Nick any of that. "One of them is to end the feud. It's gone on long enough, and too many people have been hurt."

"You always were an idealist. A fifty-year-old feud is not going to dissolve into thin air just because you want to get everyone on the same page."

He was too grounded in reality, too cynical and jaded. She mourned the hopeful, optimistic boy he once was. That person was far more likeable.

The rain whooshed down again in avalanching sheets, and Maddie white-knuckled the wheel. The clatter of the rain hitting the car roof pitched to a deafening roar.

"Maybe we should pull over?" Nick yelled over the din.

Maddie nodded and hit the flashers. She searched through the suddenly foggy windows for a spot to pull over, but the shoulder of the road was filled with a river of rushing water.

She didn't see the scattered pieces of metal in the road until it was too late. The car rumbled over the obstacles, then spun out on the wet road as one or more tires popped and blew out.

Maddie gripped the wheel hard. She managed to right the car and steer it to the side before it skittered along the gravel to a bumpy stop. The rear end of the Lexus smacked up against an iron guardrail, the only barrier between them and a pitching gully below. Suddenly the only sound was the rain that hammered the car like a volley of fireworks.

And Maddie's gasps for breath.

Calm down, calm down. She didn't want him to see her vulnerable.

"Are you okay?" Nick didn't wait for her answer. He reached over and closed his hands lightly around her arms, gently squeezing up and down, checking for something...

injury, sprains, breaks?

His bright eyes lit with concern. "Maddie, say something."

"I—I don't know what just happened—" *Don't blather.*

Nick craned his head to see out the back, but the car windows were covered with ice-like sheets of rain, blurring everything outside into fuzzy hues of gray.

"It looked like some kind of metal scraps scattered in the road," she finally said. "I—I didn't see them till too late. I'm so sorry."

"Whatever it was, you couldn't have avoided it."

She was trembling, her tough demeanor all but crumbled. She bit down hard on her lip and blinked back tears. *Please, God, not in front of him.*

He rubbed her arms up and down, as if he wanted to ease her anxiety. She didn't dare meet his eyes for fear she'd do something really stupid like melt into his big embrace and hold on for dear life. His touch felt frighteningly good, firm yet amazingly gentle.

"It's okay," he said in a calm, low voice. "We're all right. That's all that matters."

Tears leaked down her cheeks, and she swiped them away.

"It's just a car," Nick said gently.

"I've got to check the damage." She placed her hand on the door handle.

A strong but firm hand held her back. "Oh, no, you don't. We're staying right here and calling for help."

His commanding tone half irked her, but the other half was unbearably relieved he took charge.

"Are you hurt?" she asked.

"Honey, it takes more than a tumble on the side of the

road to rough me up. How about you?"

That little twang was back, and it shot an excruciating sense of comfort through her. His left hand had moved automatically to her shoulder and began massaging, rubbing her tense muscles, ironing out the tension that had accumulated in her neck and upper back. "Fine. Just a little shaken up," she said.

A moment ago she had actively disliked him, but his magic fingers and soothing tone changed her mind. He was kind and gentle, and his touch both soothed and excited her. She was just a second away from leaning into him and begging for more when he removed his hand to tap his phone.

Maddie looked around as best she could in the growing dusk, struggling to get it together. All she could see in the blur of the raindrops and the oncoming darkness were trees and mountains and highway. She tried to recall the last real exit she'd seen with gas and food and lodging, but it was so far back she couldn't even remember.

A sharp expletive cut the tense air and made her jump.

"What is it?" she asked.

"No service. Let me see your phone."

She dug it out of her purse and passed it to him.

Another expletive. "We're out in the boonies with no reception."

Just to make things worse, her stomach growled.

Nick tapped his watch. "Maybe the highway patrol will find us. Have you got a handkerchief?"

She stared at him like he'd just walked out of the Old South, and cracked a slow smile. "Um, I must have left my hankie in my reticule," she said in her best Charleston accent.

"Sarcasm's back. You must be okay." In one quick

movement, Nick peeled off his T-shirt and tossed it to her. "Here you go, ma'am."

Maddie caught the shirt and stifled a gasp. It was warm from his body heat and she could smell *him*, a heady mix of spicy cologne and his own particular scent, familiar and intoxicating. She had to restrain herself from holding it to her face and taking a whiff before she rolled down her window enough to stick out the shirt. Rain pelted the window and sprayed her arms and face before she could seal it closed.

Now he was sitting there shirtless, checking his phone. His muscles were perfectly honed, smooth hills of contour wrapped in a tanned, lean package. *Spectacular.* No wonder every female in Philly wanted him. Dear God, she was getting turned on in the middle of a roadside emergency. This had to stop.

The space was too confined, the heavy curtain of rain making the space too intimate and private. Fantasies circled her mind of peeling off more layers of clothing and going at it with reckless abandonment. Here in moonshine country, who would even find them? "This is all my fault," she said.

He made a *tsking* sound, gave her a contemplative look. "You haven't changed at all."

"What are you talking about?"

"Taking on everyone's burdens. Blaming yourself for things not in your control. Don't you ever ease up on yourself?"

She shrugged. "Old habits, I guess." Old habits of screwing up that she just couldn't shake no matter how hard she tried. Her inability to pick a decent job, for one. She'd finally done it, landed a job she loved, and now she had to give it all up to captain a sinking ship, an effort that would surely end in disaster. And she'd never get that job back.

"I appreciate that you didn't blame me."

Their eyes caught and held, like a slow motion pause. Awareness danced and crackled in the air between them. She remembered an easier time when they would've stayed and steamed up the windows.

She tore her gaze away, focused on the wet world outside. "We need to get out and walk, don't we?" she asked.

"Yes, ma'am." He grinned widely, his perfectly straight teeth gleaming white in the fast-approaching dark. "'Cause no one on this back-ass country road is ever gonna find us if we don't."

Chapter Six

"There hasn't been a car on the road for a half hour," Maddie said a while later, her tennis shoes making squishing sounds as she walked. "My pants are soaked through and I have a wedgie."

"Looks like that's not all that's soaked through." Nick cracked a smile as Maddie glanced down and quickly crossed her arms.

"At least *I* have a shirt on," she said.

"I would too if you hadn't locked the keys in the car." She looked upset, so he changed his tone. "Let's just keep walking. It's getting dark."

Suddenly, in the distance, headlights shone. Maddie ran out onto the road, waving her arms and shouting.

Nick ran out behind her and tried to subdue her enthusiasm by batting down her hands. "Be careful," he said. "What if it's someone we don't want to stop?"

"Nick, we're going to die from walking all night in the

soaking rain. Sometimes you've got to plunge in and take a chance."

"You're too trusting."

"And you're too suspicious." She pointed to the side of the car, which read MONMOUTH CROSSING POLICE. "See? We're saved!"

She linked her arm through Nick's elbow and did a happy dance as he grumbled and cast her a wary look. The car pulled up, revealing a massive man behind the wheel, with a long black beard and mustache and a hoop earring in one ear. He looked like Hagrid in a cop uniform. Or the leader of a Harley gang.

"Can you help us, Officer?" Maddie approached the window. "Our tires blew out, and we don't have cell service."

The cop put on his flashers and got out. He was at least six feet four. His right arm was tattooed with the word *Rosalie* and a large rose. "Let me see your IDs." His eyes roamed up and down Maddie's drenched body, and Nick didn't like that one bit.

Nick stepped forward, putting himself in front of her like a shield. "We locked our wallets in the car by accident."

"That right?" the officer said with a drawl.

"We just need a ride to a hotel for the night," Nick said.

"I'm happy to give y'all a ride into town. But the nearest Red Roof is sixty miles up the road."

Nick raked a hand through his hair. "Are there other options for lodging?"

With one phone call, he could summon his private pilot. In a couple of hours, they could be in a five-star hotel with a view of the Caribbean Sea sharing a fluffy white bed with five hundred thread count sheets and a dozen pillows of different density levels. He'd tug down her warm, plush robe to ply his hands through all her tense, aching muscles…

"Maybe at the pastor's. You married? Or just shackin' up?" Officer Hagrid flicked his gaze up and down, assessing their moral fiber.

"Oh, no, we're not—" Maddie began to answer.

"We're married. *Just* married, in fact." Nick grabbed Maddie by the waist and pulled her close, shooting her what he hoped was a smitten smile. For one delicious moment, her taut, cold nipples rubbed up against his chest, sending a cascade of heat rocketing through him. "On the way home to North Carolina."

"Where in North Carolina?"

"A place called Buckleberry Bend."

The officer's bushy brows rose up in interest. "They got that big berry festival every year."

"It's this weekend," Maddie said. "They've got berry pie, berry wine, berry jams and jellies…"

"Mulberry jam. A friend of mine brought me some jars a couple years back. Best I ever tasted."

"I'll make sure I send you some, Officer…" She glanced at his badge. "Jenkins."

The officer plucked out a cell phone from his breast pocket, under his shiny silver badge that read Filbert Jenkins, Monmouth P.D.

"Y'all hop in the back while I make this call."

Maddie slid with Nick into the back of the cruiser, which held the odor of stale beer and sweat. "Why did you tell him we were married?" she hissed.

"I didn't like the way he was eyeballing you."

"I can't help it if I look like a coed in a wet T-shirt

contest."

His eyes hovered over her chest, taking in perky breasts, each a perfectly sized handful. He forced his gaze back to her face, knowing he had to stop registering pure-lusty-guy look. "If I had my shirt…" He waved his hand over his chest. "I'd give it to you."

Maddie's eyes lingered over his bare torso. He saw her swallow nervously and was strangely pleased at his effect on her. "I'm sure Officer Jenkins will do his duty and take care of us despite the fact that we look a little sketch," she said.

"How is it that you can trust a complete stranger within five minutes, yet you've known me forever and don't trust me at all?"

"He's a police officer, Nick. And don't even talk to me about trusting you."

She was right. He'd walked out on her after their last night together, hadn't returned her calls, and had heavy investments in her family's company. She'd have to be seriously crazy to trust him. And yet, he wished he could tell her he would always have her back, would never abandon her to the elements. Would protect her with his life if Officer What's-His-Name decided to get fresh.

Maybe she noticed something in his expression. Or the fact that he'd gone quiet. Her big blue eyes softened for an instant, then she looked away. "I'm talking about how you're a guy and maybe you'd take advantage of the situation."

He narrowed his eyes. "Trust me, darlin', that's the last thing on my mind."

"It wasn't a year ago."

He stabbed a finger in the air at her. "*That* was mutual."

"It's also never happening again, just to set the record

straight."

"Not even thinking about it."

Visions of that white, bright imaginary hotel room came to mind. A spa tub big enough for two. Bubbles…in the water *and* in their champagne glasses. He'd slowly massage her back until all the tension was wrung out of her, and she went soft against him. Then he'd brush kisses down her neck and shoulder, gently gather up the orbs of her breasts and carefully kiss each one. As the steam crept up from the lilac-scented water, he'd work his magic until she arched her back and cried out his name on a moan.

"Nick. Nick!" Maddie was shaking him. "Officer Jenkins says his mother's got room for us."

Officer Jenkins placed his large, menacing face against the bars, sending what was left of Nick's fantasy fleeing. "I'll send for a tow truck to bring your car into town and the garage can work on fixing your tires tomorrow."

"Oh, thank you." Maddie clasped her hands together in a gesture of relief.

"Mama lives in a double-wide just out of town. My aunt's visiting with her Airstream, but tonight she's at my grandma's so you can stay there. It's small, just one bed, but it should be adequate."

Maddie frowned. "An Airstream?"

"One of those shiny aluminum trailer-campers," Nick said. The phrase *one bed* lingered in his mind. Fine for his fantasies, but in reality, something to be avoided at all costs.

"Silver bullet, canned ham, toaster-on-wheels," Officer Jenkins said.

"Oh," Maddie said. "Well, we're grateful, and we appreciate the hospitality."

"Can I talk to you, honey?" Nick asked, tugging her by the elbow. "Excuse us for a minute, Officer."

"Please tell me you are not thinking about refusing this offer," Maddie whispered.

"I think if I can get to where there's cell service, I can get us better accommodations." Maybe not the Caribbean island, but at least two rooms.

"No."

"Maddie, he wants us to stay in his aunt's camper." In a single bed. That was *not* happening.

"He's being kind. We can't be rude."

"I'm allergic to cats. If they have cats—"

"You're—wait—you're afraid."

He stiffened. "I am not afraid."

"Nervous then."

"Definitely not nervous."

"I hope you're not upset because this isn't a five-star offer. Surely you—"

"*No.* It's not that. I—"

"You what?"

Oh, shit.

She left him struggling with words and walked over to the cop car. "We just wanted to say thank you, Officer."

"Yes, thanks," Nick said from behind her because he had no choice. "We're grateful."

Grateful they'd be warm and dry, yes. Grateful he'd be trapped for an entire night in a tiny camper next to a sexy woman he still wanted more than food or a warm shower… not so much.

• • •

Doris Jenkins barreled toward them in a bright hibiscus-print moo-moo, arms open wide. "Poor things," she crooned. "Y'all must be exhausted. I started a little fire, and I've got weenies roasting."

Nick's brows rose a little—maybe he was a food snob too—but Maddie was starving and thankful to be saved from sleeping in soggy underwear on the side of an abandoned road.

The fire flickered, casting them in a ring of light, beyond which Maddie could make out faint outlines of other trailer homes. A picket fence edged a tidy flower garden scattered with lawn ornaments. She made out a few spinning propeller flowers, a painted wooden cutout of a woman bending over with petticoats in view, and a solar-powered gazing ball that cast a green glow. All colorful and interesting, like their hostess.

The meal was rounded out by pork 'n' beans, and when she found out dessert was s'mores, she nearly kissed Doris's flashy pink Crocs. Nick, looking relaxed for once, stretched out in an aluminum lawn chair and stuck his bare feet close to the fire. How unfair that a man could look so sexy roasting hot dogs.

"Are you married, Doris?" Maddie noticed a gold band on her left hand.

"Filbert Senior passed on two years ago." She waved her hands dismissively. "Now, don't go feeling sorry. Everyone should be so lucky. We had forty wonderful years."

Maddie instantly thought about her parents, who'd been married around thirty. Her father's stroke had certainly thrown a wrench in the gears of life. But her mom still brought him fresh coffee every morning, and a homemade dessert every night, which they shared as they sat together in the rehab hospital. Although for the first few weeks, her father could barely chew, and for another few, her mother had to feed him every bite.

That was love.

Maddie feared she would never find it herself. She always chose the wrong guy, someone she thought she could trust but who broke her heart anyway. Maybe it was her nature. Believing men were essentially good, like her dad, when they were immature, self-centered scoundrels who only wanted one thing.

She looked over at Nick. Heartbreaker Number One in all his handsome, robust glory.

"I do love me a good love story," Doris said. The fire was finally warming Maddie's damp feet. Doris had lent her a sweatshirt that said *Monmouth Bears Baseball 1999* and listed the players on the back. They had intimidating names like *Fireball Jenkins* and *Gargantua Jones*. "That's my favorite pastime. Reading romance novels from the library. Filbert Junior used to make fun of me, 'til he fell in love himself. Now he doesn't laugh." She sandwiched a roasted marshmallow between two graham crackers and handed it to Maddie. "I love to hear couple stories. Tell me yours."

Guilt stopped her from sinking into the chocolaty gooeyness of the s'more. Maddie couldn't concoct a lie for someone who had been only kind to them.

Doris looked from her to Nick, waiting expectantly. To Maddie's surprise, Nick sat forward, clasped his hands together, and chimed right in.

"Maddie and I met the first day of kindergarten. I fell in love with her at first sight, her little freckly face and that curly hair done up in pigtails with red ribbons. Went home that day and told my grandpa I had a girlfriend."

The s'more stuck in Maddie's throat, and she almost choked. *Red ribbons*. To match the red and white checked dress she'd picked out with her mom for her very first day of school. It had been her favorite. How on earth had he remembered?

The fire cast flickering light that caught a touch of gold in Nick's otherwise nearly black hair. It carved out and accentuated the strong planes and shadows of his face. He was as smoking hot as the fire.

A far cry from the little boy with the gelled-down cow-lick who held her hand during song time and sent her a cut-out valentine attached to a snack-size piece of Hershey bar melted from his sweaty little fist.

Maddie remembered something else. "When his family and mine found out we wanted to be friends, they made it clear it was not to be. And the next year they redistricted the school system and Nick got sent to another school." Nick's grandfather took over as manager of a competing shoe store one town over but never left the tiny home he owned across the tracks.

"Oh my stars, a Romeo-and-Juliet story. My favorite!" Doris popped another couple of marshmallows on a stick. "So why weren't you allowed to be friends? That seems cruel."

Nick gave a soft snort, his gaze distant in the fire. Even from where she sat, Maddie could see the fire glitter in his dark, daredevil eyes. He was a beautiful man, but she was not going to let this story get to her. No way.

"Longstanding feud between the Kingstons and the

Holters."

"Over money?" Doris asked. "It always comes down to money, doesn't it? Or a failed love. Or both."

Nick turned his gaze onto Maddie. It seemed to echo everything she was feeling—regret over the past and time lost to them forever. Words said, choices made, that could never be undone.

Anger seeped into her like the chill she felt from being damp for hours. Why had they allowed that damn feud so much power over their own lives? It wasn't their fight or their problem. They were just the innocent victims.

Maddie broke the silence. "Nick's great-grandfather and mine were apprentices under famous shoemakers in England who began a business together after World War II. They moved it to North Carolina back in the '50s and our grandfathers took it over in the '60s. I really don't know what drove them apart." She nodded toward Nick. "Do you?"

Nick shrugged.

"You must finish the story." Doris poked another couple of marshmallows onto a stick. "Tell me how you got your families back together."

Maddie fisted her hands, both fearing and anticipating what on earth he would say next.

Nick leaned forward. "Well, one day Maddie and I reconnected on a business trip. Met by accident, at a hotel in Atlanta. That same connection was there, wasn't it, sweetheart?"

His eyes drilled into hers, and Maddie felt a flush creep up her neck and clear into her face. Oh, they had connected, all right, in an electrifying, fireworks explosion way that was all starbursts, bells, and brilliant detonating explosives.

Maddie was suddenly hot and cold, trembling and turned on, and he wasn't even touching her. If they were alone, she wouldn't have hesitated a single second more to jump his bones.

Oh, no. She struggled to tether her runaway emotions. He was making up a story, and she was buying into his bullshit. That was a recipe for disaster. How the hell was she going to spend the night in that little camper-thingie with him?

"So what on earth happened?" Doris literally sat on the edge of her canvas outdoor chair.

Maddie cleared her throat. She sucked in a big, deep breath. But no words formed.

Nick cleared his throat. "Yes, well, our families saw our happiness and decided to end their feud."

Nick stood and placed his arms on his hips, assuming the tone and inflection of an actor. He was good. Really good. "I took Maddie back home and I said, 'Gramps, Maddie's the love of my life. Now, I know you haven't been talking to your old friend, and our families completely ignore one another when they pass on the street, but time's up and that baloney's got to end.' Then I took her in my arms like this— " Nick pulled Maddie up, grabbed her around the waist and dipped her low— "and I said, 'Sweetheart, it's up to you and me to bring our families back together. Full circle. 'Cause that's what love does.'"

He eased her up slowly, the taut cords of his arm muscles pulling, pulling. His warm brown eyes stared into hers, and she went limp under his touch. He smelled of campfire and fresh air. His lips hovered so close she could feel his breath on her cheek. Just when she thought he would kiss her, she landed upright, and he sat back down in his chair, snagging another s'more from the platter.

Dear God. Maddie stood with knees wobbling, breaths shaky and shallow. As she hitched down the sweatshirt and righted herself, Maddie wondered what kind of power Nicholas Holter possessed that his one touch could send her swirling into a melted puddle? She was so doomed. Worse, she was incapable of hating him, even though he was a vulture capitalist scoundrel who would take her whole family down if she couldn't buck up and face him.

Doris clutched her heart. "True love prevails! Oh, I knew it. You two were meant to be. *Destiny.*"

Her marshmallows burst into brilliant orange flame, and Doris blew and sputtered and waved them in the air.

The strange spell that had been cast burst as well. In their real story, there was no hope, no destiny. No expectations that love could conquer all the bad stuff in life. There was just Nick's bitter desire for revenge against the company that he felt sold his grandfather down the river.

Maddie pulled a smoking marshmallow off Doris's stick and popped it into her mouth. It was charred and burned and crispy on the outside. Just like her heart.

Real life didn't turn out like a fairy tale, no matter how badly she wanted it to. It wouldn't bring her true love, or get her father's health back, or stop this sexy, irresistible man from ruining her family. And the reality of knowing that really sucked.

• • •

After helping Doris clean up, Nick followed Maddie to the

tiny Airstream and locked the door behind them. Walking through its shiny aluminum door was like entering a flying saucer from an old sci-fi movie.

He was expecting retro décor, not circa-1970s-time-warp, from the orange vinyl banquette to the green shaggy rug, to the brown and gold curtains at the windows. The smell of this morning's coffee lingered in the air. Their two duffle bags squatted in the aisle, compliments of Doris's son.

When he turned from double-checking the door, he found Maddie staring at him. Finally, he caved. "What is it?" He hoped she wasn't going to interrogate him about that crazy story he'd told around the fire.

"I never realized you were so OCD."

"I like order and safety. What's wrong with that?" Truthfully, he *was* sort of OCD, especially when the safety of people he cared for was at stake. But sometimes he craved dangerous and out of control. Like he knew it would be with her.

"That surprises me," she said. "Don't you skydive?"

He shrugged, noting with a shot of dread there really was only one bed. "I have, a time or two."

"And you fly your own plane."

"Just for pleasure."

Other things he'd like to do for pleasure swirled around his head uninvited. Like dragging his hands through that luscious, crazy-curly hair of hers, inhaling its usual lemony essence, letting the silky locks run like water through his fingers. How the hell was he going to sleep in this tiny sardine can so near to her and not lose it?

He should never have touched her by the fire. He'd pulled her up to be funny and dramatic and to entertain Doris. But

Maddie's T-shirt had slid up and the soft, forbidden skin of her waist slid under his hands, pliant and velvety. He'd been one heartbeat away from pulling her close and devouring her plush pink lips.

Whew. All that from one whopper of a tall tale. Why had he done it? To be honest, it wasn't just to entertain their host. Telling the story had pleased him in some primordial way, navigated their family complexities in such a way that made it actually seem possible for them to be together.

This was all his fault for telling Doris's son they were married. Feeling protective of Maddie had gotten him nowhere but trapped in this tiny trailer with all his erotic fantasies charging full force forward like the bulls in Pamplona.

Since when was he such a sucker for fairy tale endings?

No such thing in real life. He'd already all but bought out that stupid company. His granddad was seventy-two, and this would be his last shot to chase and capture the dream that had always been just out of his reach.

When all was said and done, Maddie would never forgive him for booting her dad and his longtime staff. Taking over Kingston Shoes would be the final string that would unravel and cut them off from one another for good.

Maddie looked around at the tiny sink, opened the bathroom door. "This might not be a luxury accommodation like you're used to, but it's clean and cute, in a retro way."

He gave a nonchalant shrug. "It's adequate." He hated pretending to be a snob. The Filberts were good, kind people. But how else was he going to keep up the wall between them?

"Whatever. I like it." Maddie placed her duffle bag on the table and began digging through it. "I'm going to take a shower."

The bathroom door closed, and the water turned on. Nick looked down at the carpet. A scrap of bright pink lace lay there forgotten. He bent down and scooped it up— Maddie's panties.

His brain instantly flashed back to their night together, where nothing was enough, not the deep wet kisses or the frantic crazed touches. He'd never wanted another woman more. Yet there'd been something else between them, something over and above the lust that boiled in his blood for her, but he had no words for those more dangerous feelings. He'd learned from the tragedy in his past to keep his heart close, to put all his drive into succeeding at business where the risks were far less. His response was to lower his mouth to hers and devour her instead.

He sat at the orange vinyl banquette, fingering the panties. She had lace ones that night too, just a filmy strip of black. He'd slipped his fingers under that lace, dipped into a dream that had haunted him for years and years.

"What the hell are you doing with my underwear?"

Startled, he jumped up and dropped it, feeling worse than a kid caught sneaking Halloween candy.

Maddie stood before him, dripping and wrapped in a faded Budweiser beach towel that left a long expanse of toned legs and pretty feet exposed for his perusal.

Nick didn't ever blush, but now blood whooshed into his face. But he kept his response flippant. "I don't have this color in my collection." He set the underwear on the back of the couch and dug through his own duffle. "I'll go next."

He strategized his next move. He could admit he was turned on and horny and wanted her. Bad. They could share the bed; forget all about blown out tires, and road trips, and pissed off grandpas, and companies going down the tubes. He opened his mouth to speak, but she cut him off at the pass.

"We should flip for the bed," she said.

"No. You have it. I'm good on—that." *That* was a breakfast banquette, half his size at most. He gathered up his toothbrush and dental floss, but she blocked his entrance to the bathroom.

"Why'd you do it?"

"Do what?" He hoped she wasn't going to ask him if he had a panty fetish.

"You know—make up that ending for Doris at the campfire."

Water dripped off spiral curls and onto her smooth, sleek shoulders. He wanted to pull one out straight with his fingers just to watch it spring back. The scent of shampoo caught in his nostrils—evergreen fresh.

She held a death grip on the towel, but what would happen if he moved forward, just a little? What if he placed his hand over hers, drew her close, and let the towel slip silently to the floor?

He swallowed hard, forced his brain to answer the question. "She needed a happy ending. But I don't believe in fairy tales like you do."

Her voice was so low he could barely hear. "Don't you ever wonder what would have happened if things with our families were different?"

All the time. "There's no use reimagining the past. Too many people have been hurt already."

"But what about a year ago—between us?"

"Are you saying you want to sleep with me?"

Shit, what had he just said? He'd just blurted that out with zero charm or tact. He could have rephrased it a thousand better ways. Better, he should have used his lips and hands to ask instead of his big mouth.

"Absolutely not. Of course not. NO." She paused, groping for words. "But we used to be friends. Best friends. And what you said by the fire — "

He couldn't remember what he'd said by the fire. All he could think of was how turned on he was, how being in her presence for any length of time drove his hormones batshit crazy. Making love with her had been fantastic, the best night of his life. How much of these close quarters could a red-blooded man take anyway? He was certain she was feeling the pull too. Why not indulge for one more night?

"I'll take my underwear back now."

Nick heard her but some perverse part of his brain refused to comply. As she reached for them, he scooped them up, dangling them before her face. "No."

Her eyes flew open wide. "Give. Me. Back. My. Underwear."

He laughed, a deep, hearty laugh that loosened everything inside, including what remained of his common sense. "Guess you'll just have to come get them."

She snatched at the panties on tiptoe, but he yanked them just out of her reach, her soft breasts pushing against him as she frantically attempted to grasp the tiny slip of material. The scent of generic white soap clung to her soft skin, and it smelled better than the exotic, expensive Italian fragrance next to his bathroom sink. They had nearly backed up against the bed when she tackled him, tumbling both of them backwards and straddling him until she finally grabbed hold of her prize.

She was panting, her wild curly hair dripping wet and tumbling around her shoulders. Her breasts, barely contained by the towel, fell soft and lush before his eyes. Her focus was solely on her goal, until their eyes met and gazes locked. He saw the exact moment when their situation dawned on her. In the second before she could scramble off him, he reached up and planted his lips over hers. She gasped raggedly, but he snaked a hand behind her neck and pulled her closer, slipping his tongue in her mouth and kissing her deep and hard.

She collapsed into the kiss, giving him back as much as he took. Something snapped inside him. In one quick motion, he rolled them over and pinned her to the mattress. Their bodies melted together, separated only by the thin towel and the length of his raging erection.

His mouth possessed her. Her lips parted on a sigh, and he took full advantage, thrusting his tongue into the hot recesses of her mouth, capturing and devouring hers with his. Instinctively, he reached for her breast, rubbing his fingers over a taut nipple until she moaned deep in her throat and pushed against him.

The towel clung between their bodies, a thin fragment of cloth. Now was the time to think, be sensible, back off. Nick fisted the fabric. A second passed like an eternity. Then he tugged until it pulled free.

Maddie lay naked before him, her wet wild hair tumbled around her face, beautiful curves displayed before him like a statue of a goddess, her triumphant expression on claiming her underwear replaced by a haze of desire.

She was so beautiful. Too beautiful for him, because she

was beautiful on the inside as well as out, and he was just a damaged shell who had no idea how to love a woman for keeps. Before he could think any further, Nick yanked off his shirt, tossed it on the floor with the towel, and gathered her up against him.

His body ached for her, and judging from the way she was responding, she felt the same. Maybe this long road fiasco wasn't so bad after all, if it allowed them to be together for one night, to steal the pleasure they both wanted so badly.

Just as she tugged at his shorts, a rap sounded on the door. Nick tore his lips from Maddie's lush breast and moved to the door as she dove to retrieve the towel.

Nick inhaled a few deep breaths and combed his fingers through his hair, trying to look presentable before he yanked open the door. Doris stood there, holding his cell phone. "Thought you might be needing this."

He'd been so distracted by Maddie at the campfire that he'd forgotten his link to civilization. Nick thanked Doris and took a minute to walk her to her door across the way. He needed the time to calm down and start thinking with something other than his dick.

What the hell was he doing? He'd forgotten his mission, which was to take over her family's business and put his grandfather in charge. If he slept with Maddie, emotions would get tangled, and he'd be obligated to back down on the business. The injustice done to his grandfather would never be righted. He could not choose another one-nighter with her—no matter how mind-blowingly sensational—over his honor, his family.

When he re-entered the camper, Maddie was dressed in boxer briefs and a T-shirt, rummaging intently through her cosmetics bag.

Nick quietly shut the door behind him and leaned against it. She didn't even look up so he spoke. "That was a… mistake." He announced it like one of his pronouncements at a business meeting. Cool, rational, and deadly.

"Yes, of course," she said but he'd seen her cringe, just as surely as if he'd caused her physical pain. She scoured his face for a sign that he was lying, or kidding, or *something*, but he kept his expression neutral.

He gave his best I-don't-give-a-flying shrug. "We were just messing around, and I got carried away. Close quarters and all."

She yanked the blanket off the bed. "You can take the bed," she said, then threw it down on the hard, short banquette.

He should have let it go, let her go, but his heart compelled him to act, and he flew after her in two barefoot strides. His arm caught her elbow and whirled her toward him.

Her eyes glinted with anger; he saw it even in the dim light. It was hard, even now, not to gather her up and kiss her senseless, drag her down onto the bed and not come up until he'd finished exploring every last curve and valley.

His muscles actually trembled. Why was he always a flash of a second away from losing control with her? Like that one fine night when they couldn't keep their hands off each other. Years and years of bound up feelings finally let loose. For that one and only time, he'd felt a glimmer of hope that maybe the past didn't predict the future, that there really was forgiveness and mending and fresh chances.

But that had only lasted until the phone rang at dawn.

Maddie stood there staring at him. His hand still clung to her arm as though he feared she would bolt like a scared rabbit out of the camper and into the woods. She shrugged it briskly away. "Business is business, right, Nick? From now on, let's just keep everything else out of it."

She thought he was unfeeling, some kind of sociopath who pulled family businesses out from under people for pleasure. She couldn't have been more wrong.

His gaze locked on hers. Raw emotion registered, lust and sadness and torment, and for a raw, brutal instant, Nick felt it all run through his heart like a blade.

He did feel, and she had no idea how much.

He tugged the blanket from her hands. "I'm taking the seat. Good night."

As soon as this god-awful weekend was done, he'd force himself to forget her. It would be easy, because she'd hate him for real when all was said and done.

Chapter Seven

Two wet, naked cowboys tore around the corner of the blue-shuttered, two story colonial at the end of Morning Glory Lane. Maddie turned off the ignition of the Honda Accord that, thanks to Nick, had magically appeared outside of Doris's at eight a.m. and had gotten them to Buckleberry Bend by lunchtime. She took a moment to enjoy the look on Nick's face, which was a cross between *please-God-can-I-go-home* and *no-one-told-me-I-had-to-deal-with-children-this-weekend-too*.

She'd slept poorly in the camper, and it had nothing to do with the comfort of the bed. She knew he'd tossed and turned most of the night too. Today during the drive they'd kept the conversation sterile and innocuous. It would be a relief to be with her family and get some libido-killing distance between them. Nothing would happen if she played it safe and didn't lead them into any untoward situations.

"Maddie, look, about last night…"

She turned and tried not to look into his intense brown eyes, tried not to remember how they'd flamed with desire when he'd fisted that towel and whisked it away like an artist revealing a prized painting. "Close quarters, romantic firelight stories…our hormones just ran away from us."

"It would be wrong to let our physical attraction for each other get in the way of business," he said.

"I agree. Besides, my posse's here to protect me if you try something like that again."

Nick's face wore a look of sheer panic. "Your what?"

"Don't worry…" Maddie said as the little boys ran yelling and screaming up to the car. "They're only three." The cowboys smacked their hands on the windows, one on each side. "On second thought, those squirt guns *might* be loaded."

Maddie ran out of the car and scooped up the first blond-haired little boy. The straw cowboy hat drifted off as she twirled him in the air, and he shrieked with laughter. "Hi, Alex." She kissed him on top of his sun-warmed head.

"You're wet!" she said, putting him down.

"And nekked!" he said.

"Yes, you are at that."

"Aunt Maddie, Aunt Maddie!" his brother Logan cried as he plowed forward and wrapped his own dripping wet self around Nick's leg.

"Not Aunt Maddie," Nick said with relief as he reluctantly patted the mass of blond curls.

Nick stood a little stiffly, looking like he wished he were anywhere else. Precisely how Maddie wanted him to feel. Maybe his conscience hadn't completely flown the coop.

Alex tugged on Nick's cargo shorts. Heartbreaker blue

eyes looked up and took everything in. "Are you Aunt Maddie's boyfwend?"

Logan, always discriminating, didn't wait for an answer. He drew his gun and stared shooting.

The water pelted Nick in the neck. Nick shot Maddie a glance that said, *who is this kid? Devil's spawn?*

Maddie shrugged. "They're not usually this wound up. They must be excited."

The next round hit her in the middle of her T-shirt.

The perpetrator giggled a madcap laugh, delighted and perverse as any deranged criminal.

"Okay, Squirt. You are *so* going to get it." Maddie kicked off her flip-flops and charged toward the little shooter, whooping up her best battle cry. The little boy screamed and dropped his gun, then darted toward the rear of the house with Maddie in full pursuit.

Footsteps pounded behind her. When she glanced back, it wasn't Alex but Nick, dangling buck-naked Alex upside down over his shoulder, both of them hollering right along through the tree-covered yard.

For the second time in two days, Nick's laughter caught her off guard. Effusive, contagious. *Fun.* Something she hadn't had in quite a while.

"Daddy, daddy, daddy!" Logan squealed. Rounding the corner to the backyard, Maddie saw the puzzled expression on her older brother Derrick's face as he sat up in his lawn chair, his newspaper scattering on the breeze. Logan jumped into a baby pool and waded through it before catapulting himself into his father's arms.

"Aunt Maddie's attacking me," he fake whined.

Maddie reached the pool, which had pictures of red and

blue cartoon fish emblazoned on the bottom. She reached across to grab Logan but lost her balance and slipped on the smooth latex bottom, landing on her butt in the middle.

Logan giggled.

"Okay, you're gonna get it!" She stood, dripping wet, and swooped up her nephew, taking him down with her into the shallow pool. Alex tore away from Nick's arms and jumped in after them.

"Let's splash Aunt Maddie!" one of them screamed.

Before she could cry foul play, Logan and Alex thrashed around the pool, stirring up enough water to create a small tsunami while Nick supplied them with water toys.

"You all are ganging up on me!" she said through a curtain of water that was splashed and kicked at her by tiny hands and feet going full force. "This is *not* fair."

In self-defense, she grabbed hold of Logan's squirt gun and blasted Nick in the chest. A wicked glint in his eyes, he scooped up a bucket full of water and dumped it on her head.

The shock of icy water cascading onto her hair and flowing down her back momentarily paralyzed her. But she wouldn't be able to live with herself if he got off scot-free. So she pretended outrage, standing in the middle of the pool and flapping her hands. Just when Nick thought the fight was over, she stepped out and gave him a full body hug, plastering her sopping wet self against him.

Her intent was to make him wet. Make him pay as she splashed waves of water onto his fine Italian loafers, pressed her wet head solidly against his cheek and wrapped her arms around his premium polo.

"Whoa there, what are you—" His body tensed in

surprise and shock. His arm went protectively around her waist to prevent them from toppling. Their gazes locked and Maddie froze for she wasn't sure how long. She found herself staring into eyes containing fascinating shades of chestnut and cocoa and lovely little golden flecks she'd never noticed before. Tiny little crinkles gathered in the outside corners, a maturing trait that made him a thousand times sexier than when he was younger.

She was chilled and hot at the same time. Her heart knocked against her chest loud enough to block out the noises of the little boys' laughter. She'd meant only to make him sufficiently wet to pay for his bad deeds. Except now it seemed as though *she* were the one paying.

She looked away, and her gaze lit on his wrist. "Your Rolex is wet. Is it ruined?"

He wiped it on his pants, which were damp. "Nah, it's pretty indestructible."

Her brother cleared his throat. "Alex, Logan! Out now to dry off before your mother gets home!"

The screen door to the house slammed.

"What on earth is going on here?"

Maddie looked up to see the most elegant woman south of the Mason-Dixon line looking like a Talbot's ad tapping her red pumps, showing off her still-trim figure in red capri pants and a navy sleeveless blouse.

"Gran!" Grandmother Amelia, she'd wanted to be called, but that had quickly gotten shortened to Grandmeel when they were kids since no one could say such a heinous mouthful.

"Madison?" Grandmeel's steely gaze took in her dripping wet hair, soggy clothes, and bare feet.

It shouldn't have hurt that her own grandmother didn't move to hug her. "Oh. I—I'm sorry, Gran." That awful word *screwup* echoed in her mind. She should have made a more proper entrance, and she'd acted like one of the little kids instead.

Nick had crossed his arms and wore a dark frown. Either he was bristling at her undignified behavior or her grandmother's iciness, she couldn't tell. Or maybe he sensed he'd be the next to fall under her scrutiny.

The boys flopped out of the pool like wet fish and bounded to their mother, who stood next to her grandmother, holding a towel for each of them.

"Hey, Jenna." Maddie waved, remembering to suction-extract her wet T-shirt from her skin before anyone commented. Out of the corner of her eye, she caught Nick staring. *Too late.* Oh, well, her face was already red from Grandmeel's disapproval.

Fortunately, Jenna spoke. "Derrick, why are these boys naked as newborns? And I'm sure you failed to put sunblock on their nether regions."

"Daddy told us to be naked and proud," Logan said.

"Nekked and pwoud," echoed his cohort in crime.

Jenna rolled her eyes, but bit back a smile.

Maddie had never seen her big brother, the two hundred twenty-pound Army Captain fresh from Fort Bragg, look sheepish. "I'm sorry, baby," he told his wife. "I must've dozed off for a sec, and when I woke up, they'd taken off their suits and were streaking around the yard."

"Enough apologizing. Let's get this mayhem under control." Grandmeel waved her hands about like she was conducting a symphony. Maddie swallowed past an obstruction lodged in her throat. This was not the homecoming she'd imagined, with her mom and dad and sister and brother welcoming her lovingly into their arms. Nick would see the loving tenderness they all had for one another, agree to stop pursuing their company like a rabid dog, and mission would be accomplished. She wasn't that naïve, but she'd at least hoped her family would appear sort of normal.

Gran stepped carefully on the lawn, avoiding placing her shiny red shoes in any wet spots. Her perfectly made-up face turned as bright red as her lipstick as she came to a halt in front of them and turned to Maddie. "Why in God's name would you bring a Holter here?"

Nick bristled but cast a weary eye over Amelia's outraged form. Maddie spoke quickly to diffuse the bomb about to blow.

"Um, because we're friends, Gran. Nick is here to…give us some ideas about the company. He specializes in business financial planning."

Business decimation more likely, but of course she couldn't say *that*.

"A pleasure to see you again, Mrs. Kingston," he said with a surprisingly relaxed grin. But Amelia Scarlett O'Hanlon Kingston was having none of it. She looked like she'd been bitten by a snake….and the venom was spreading.

Her usually cool grandmother looked shaken. "You are the spitting image of your grandfather when he was your age."

Maddie feared she was going to reach out and touch Nick's face. She studied every feature carefully, as if she didn't trust her own senses. As if she were seeing a mirage.

At last she turned to Maddie. "Madison, you've shown

your usual poor judgment in bringing this traitor into our midst. Surely, he can stay in town at the bed and breakfast."

"Amelia, come cool off with some sweet tea." Maddie's mother ran out of the house with a tray containing a pitcher of tea with bobbing lemon slices and a huge plate of cookies. Maddie could bet the business they were warm, too. Mom baked when she was stressed, and Amelia had always been a continual burr in her sneaker.

Her mom wore a frilly pink and green apron over jean shorts and flip-flops. She brushed an errant curl off her forehead as she stepped down onto the deck.

A big black-and-white dog bounded alongside her.

"Hughie!" Madison ran forward to embrace the dog she'd rescued her senior year in high school and soon found herself covered with licks and kisses. Hughie could always be counted on to provide the affection Grandmeel lacked.

Amelia spoke to Maddie's mother. "I thought you were at the hosp—"

"Well, I'm back now," Rosalyn Kingston quickly but cheerily cut her off. "C'mon, everyone, let's have some refreshments."

Maddie ran to take the tray from her mother, but Nick had already set it on the wrought-iron patio table. She hugged and kissed her mother and exchanged a look that said, "one disaster averted."

Too bad there were too many to count ahead.

"Don't worry. I've spiked her tea," her mother whispered in the sweetest southern drawl ever. No one would suspect this gentle, unassuming woman doubled as a badass judge on the county's district court.

"Nicholas. It's been way too long." Despite him being

wet, Maddie's mother enveloped him in a warm hug Maddie hoped would erase her grandmother's cold welcome. Even if Nick was a rat at heart, he'd fulfilled his side of the bargain and didn't deserve to be treated inhospitably.

Rosalyn held him at arm's length, studying him like a mom checks for drips of ice cream on her toddler's chin. "Let me have a look at you. My, you've grown up handsome. And Maddie tells me you're quite successful. Your grandfather must be so proud."

"Mrs. K." Nick positively beamed under her scrutiny. Another surprise. Maddie recalled her mother always had a soft spot for Nick, but this was the first time she saw the feeling was absolutely mutual.

Amelia scowled at the show of affection and grudgingly took a drink.

Maddie was grateful for her mother's kindness and gave her a big squeeze to prove it. "Madison. My baby," her mother crooned, and Maddie found herself the current object of her mother's encompassing affection. "We are so excited to see you and so delighted Nick is here. In my opinion, it's about time."

Maddie started to say "Mom, we're just friends—" but the words died in the crush of her embrace. She marveled at her strong mother, who had handled Dad's illness mostly on her own these past months.

"It's so wonderful to have you kids home this weekend. Too bad Liz couldn't make it."

"At least she has a great excuse." Her overachieving big sister was off eradicating polio in West Africa with Doctors Without Borders. Liz had signed up right after her divorce finalized six months ago, eager to leave the tiny town where she couldn't help but run into her police chief ex at every turn.

"How long are you here for, Nick?" Derrick came forward to shake Nick's hand. Nick raked back his wet hair before he extended his own hand. Despite the fact that he was pretty much soaked from his head to the toes of his expensive soggy loafers, he seemed remarkably composed.

"Just for the weekend."

"Well, we appreciate your trying to help Madison with this crazy scheme of hers."

Maddie turned to Derrick. "What crazy scheme?"

"You know. Taking over the company without any business experience." He turned to Nick. "I told her we should have let Al take the helm, but she's so stubborn—"

"Derrick, please." Maddie held up a hand to halt the verbal diarrhea. Uncle Al was pushing seventy. He'd done everything possible to keep the company afloat. All he wanted to do now was enjoy his grandkids and fish every day. He deserved to, and the company deserved a fresh start.

And by default, that happened to be with her at the helm.

"Well, you haven't exactly had a track record of success—"

Maddie clenched her hands into fists. Knowing her brother, he was going to illustrate his point with Crayola-colored examples of her past incompetence. She would not stand here like she was thirteen and suffer through it.

"I have a great job now, Derrick."

"*Had* is what I heard."

She took a sip of tea, wishing she had what Grandmeel was having. "I've made some difficult decisions, but I believe they're good ones."

He snorted. "Yeah. Like the website design start-up that failed after you borrowed money from Mom and Dad. Or that deadbeat rodeo wrangler."

Oh, God, no. Okay, so the start-up had tanked, but she'd paid every penny back. But why did he have to bring up her failed engagement from a year and a half ago? Maddie's face heated. Derrick was playing dirty, in front of Nick. Why now? *Especially* now, when she needed solidarity and support from her family.

Nick's brow raised in a question, but maybe also in judgment. Soon he'd know all about her past mishaps and mistakes, and he'd gloat too.

Derrick took a swig of beer and sighed heavily. "I'm sorry, but I think you're foolish to quit the best job you've ever had to come back home and try to run the business. You need to find someone more competent, or we're just going to lose it all."

Maddie looked at her mother. She was biting the inside of her cheek, a sure sign that she was upset. Maddie needed to be mature and change the topic before the truth came out about her dad, but her tongue seemed stuck to the roof of her mouth. Why, oh why was she one of these people that thought of snappy comebacks and shutdowns two hours late?

Before Maddie could un-velcro her tongue, Nick spoke. "Actually, I believe Maddie's more than qualified to step in, and she's got a good plan. Trouble is, even the best plan may not be enough at this point to save the business."

Whoa. Say what? Nick had just defended her. Shut down her bully brother. Wow. The enemy wasn't so…enemous.

Maddie's mom gave Derrick a little shove. "Why don't

you go help Jenna with the boys?"

Derrick frowned at Maddie but did as their mother said.

"I think your grandmother is right," Nick said. "I'm happy to get a room at the B and B."

Grandmeel gave an I-told-you-so smirk, but Maddie's mom patted Nick on the back. "You'll stay with us. We positively wouldn't have it any other way. Now let's sit and enjoy these cookies while they're fresh out of the oven."

Maddie handed Nick a sweet tea and a cookie, which he took with a huge grin. Despite her resolve, it made her feel all melty inside—just like the chocolate chips—and helped erase some of her embarrassment at her family's antics.

As she sat on her parents' deck, a voice in her head niggled. *This is not real.* Nick was not here to offer advice or to analyze where the business was turning south. He was here because she'd paid for him to be, with all her money and some of Cat's. She could not allow herself to get lulled into thinking otherwise.

Grandmeel with all her iciness was the only one with a real handle on this wacky situation. Yet Maddie's heart rebelled, begging to get caught up in the fantasy.

That was what had always gotten her into trouble in the past. Her stupid heart, so quick to trust and believe. Her family would shake their heads and think, *There she goes again. Following her impulses instead of her sense.*

Maddie knew that heart could not be trusted. She looked over at her grandmother and tried to adopt her same strict posture. If she didn't shove that same steel rod up her backside, she would ruin the one chance she had to save her family.

The little boys greedily grabbed for cookies, and Jenna

gave them each a juice box. Maddie noticed they now wore swim trunks as they padded across the deck in their bare feet to sit in the corner near a pile of action figures and toy cars. Hughie, smart dog that he was, eagerly followed the trail of cookie crumbs behind them.

The tea tasted like home, the cookies were comforting in their warm deliciousness, and Maddie finally felt herself relaxing.

Until Derrick spoke again. "So, are you two back together?" He always was as subtle as an eighteen-wheeler blasting around the curves of a mountainous West Virginia highway.

"No, we are not." Maddie decided to stomp this one down fast before it grew into a disaster. "Nick is here to see his grandfather."

"Well, I remember *that thing* you two had in high school."

Ah, yes, *that thing*. That combustible, explosive thing that flared and burst brighter and louder than fireworks over New York Harbor. And left her heart charred and shattered for years.

Derrick stood, probably just to intimidate further. "Just to be clear, Nick can sleep in the family room."

Who did Derrick think he was, anyway, her father? Suddenly the reason for his bad cop routine became more obvious. Maybe he was trying to step in for Dad. In his usual blunt scary way. It was half touching and half horrifying.

"I'll sleep anywhere," Nick said, unfazed. "Couch, floor, anything's fine."

Derrick slapped Nick on the back a little too hard. "Just not in my sister's bed."

Maddie choked on her sweet tea. She used the coughing

and sputtering as an excuse to head into the house for a real drink.

Where the hell was the scotch? It had always been in the liquor cabinet in the family room, but her mom must have moved it out of reach of the little kids. She headed to the tiny pantry off the kitchen, where she strained on tiptoes to wrap her fingers around the bottle.

"Want me to reach that for you?" a familiar masculine voice asked from the pantry doorway.

Nick.

He leaned casually against the painted doorframe, arms crossed, biceps in full view. Seeing him all strong and tall and handsome, relaxed and still half wet, fired up a hormone storm inside her that made her want to do something really crazy like wrap her body around his hard toned one and drag him down among the Diet Coke cans and the tin of dog biscuits without a second thought.

Funny how your own family could make you want to run screaming into the arms of the enemy.

"Only if you'll join me." She tried to sound cool and in control but she was anything but.

"Oh, I'd love to join you." He flashed a devilish grin that made her pulse jump and stepped up close behind her in the tight space to reach over her head. She vaguely registered the bag of flour at eye level because most of her focus was on the hard muscular body pressing her into the shelf.

"Hurry up," she said, mainly to distract herself. "I need it fast before my mom discovers I'm drinking in the closet."

Nick was in no hurry. His left hand skimmed down her arm as his right grabbed the scotch bottle from the shelf. She felt his wet shirt and his belt buckle press into her back. "I can give it to you fast," he whispered low and throaty. "Help you release all that pent-up tension."

Dear God, did he really just say that? Before she could protest, his hand snaked to the back of her neck. The shock of his touch made every nerve ending stand on end. His fine, long-fingered hands massaged her neck gently, expertly, and oh, my, he had magic hands. Even better than alongside the highway. Within ten seconds she wanted to loll her head backward and moan from sheer pleasure. He kneaded between her shoulder blades, diffused the tightness in her trapezius, her shoulders, her neck. Slowly her mind stopped replaying the horrendous scenes from a few minutes ago.

"So tense." Nick *tsked*, as if he had just the remedy to fix it.

She could only nod like a boneless heap of jelly under his pliant fingers.

"Take a deep breath. You handled them well."

"Why are you…" She shook her head against the haze of lust. "Why are you doing this?"

She turned around so he had to break contact. She stood with her hands behind her, gripping onto the pantry shelf. He was very close, his eyes darkly twinkling, molten with desire.

In the kitchen, the screen door slammed. Hughie barked. Voices and laughter followed.

Nick handed her the bottle of scotch and shrugged. "Guess you'll have to wait for later."

"For what?" she asked groggily.

"For more massaging. Or that drink. Or for whatever else you might need." He turned and left, leaving her breathless and shaking.

Maddie pulled off the cap and took a drink from the bottle, wiping her mouth with the back of her hand as she let herself slide slowly down the pantry wall.

Yep, she had her hands full with her family and with the business she'd come here to lead. Nick was supposed to be the enemy, yet he'd handled Grandmeel and Derrick and stood up for her in front of her family. Then he'd offered her—what?—comfort and humor and oh, hell, the best damn massage she'd ever had.

How was it that the one man who could take their company down appeared to be the only one who seemed to believe in her?

She stood and struggled for sanity, gave herself a good hard smack on the forehead. Getting turned on in the pantry by the man that was going to ruin her family was really bad. Almost as bad as ever thinking bringing him home was a good idea.

Chapter Eight

Okay, the pantry was a mistake.

Nick should have stayed outside. He could handle himself with the Relatives from Hell. Besides he'd always liked Maddie's mom.

Except Maddie got to him. He'd felt her pain, standing up to her grandmother and brother. She was doing her best in a bad situation, and he'd felt an overwhelming urge to comfort her, make her laugh. Kiss her until she forgot all about her crazy family and all the insane pressure she was under. She needed defenders. Hell, where was her father?

He reminded himself again to keep it professional. He'd let his emotions override his sense again, as seemed to happen whenever he was around her.

An hour later, the idea of having dinner with his grandfather sounded like the perfect escape. Plus, he needed to complete his mission—put his grandfather in charge and be done with this once and for all. Nick drove through the tiny town. Downtown Buckleberry Bend was decked out for the Berry Festival like a present wrapped and decorated for a special occasion. Banners looped languidly across Main Street and colorful flowers burst out of baskets hung from the wrought iron lampposts.

Vendor booths were set up in the park and all the shop windows were adorned with red, white, and blue—the pancake house, the five-and-dime, the antique shops and small art galleries, the main store for Kingston Shoes. Even the coffee shop where all the old-timers ate breakfast and hung out in rocking chairs all afternoon displayed enticing wares for the street traffic.

Nick stopped at the B and B to inquire about a room, but they were booked for the holiday. Maybe he would stay with his grandfather, just text Maddie it was better that way. He needed to get some distance between the two of them before he did something really stupid. Under the same roof and just a set of stairs away, God knew what could happen.

The shops soon ended, replaced on the outskirts of the town by the shoe factory and farmland where the corn was knee high. Nick drove across railroad tracks to the tiny neighborhood where he grew up.

The car crunched up the gravel drive to the side of a little white box of a house set behind a garden of blooming geraniums. An American flag hung proudly from the front porch. Behind the wheel, Nick scrubbed his hands over his face. This place held a mixed basket of memories, good and bad, but tugging in his mind was a persistent thought that had nothing to do with his upbringing.

The rodeo wrangler.

He resisted the urge to call one of his men, send him to

Texas, and punch that all-talk-no-work cowboy right in his gleaming bleached teeth.

Why did Nick ever agree to come back here? He could take the condescending brother and the suspicious grandma, but it seemed Maddie frightened him most of all. No other woman had ever made him feel like that.

The day she was supposed to get married, he'd gotten drunk, sat around all day watching football and washing down salsa and chips with beer. Then he went and broke up with his girlfriend-at-the-time. That was probably the only good thing he did that day. He'd had a fiendish impulse to hop in his car, drive to North Carolina, and tell Maddie all the things he should have said long ago. Only common sense stopped him, and the fact that he was too damned drunk to drive.

Nick shook his head hard to clear it. Nostalgia did that to you. Ripped out your guts and forced you to remember things best left covered with cobwebs in the very back of your mind. Seeing Gramps would be just the thing to get his mind straight and drive thoughts of Maddie from his mind. His grandfather, after all, was the reason he'd invested in Kingston Shoes in the first place.

"Well I'll be a son of a—"

Samuel Holter's imposing figure filled the doll-house doorway, but Nick wasn't intimidated. He was just as tall and broad. The two could have been father and son instead of two generations apart.

"Wish you'd let me replace that damn unsafe rust bucket in the driveway," Nick grumbled. He hugged him even though he knew Gramps wasn't much into physical contact. His grandfather eyeballed him up and down like an astute mother capturing every detail of her prodigal child come home.

"Want some dinner?" His grandfather tossed the words over his shoulder as he moved into the house.

"I'll take a beer if you have one."

The living room was tidy but sparse, exactly as Nick remembered it—a dull brown La-Z-Boy chair with a couple empty Coke cans strewn on a small table, a beat-up old couch, plain walls hung with cheap landscape paintings of lakes. The only change was the giant-screen TV in the corner—a gift from Nick last Christmas.

"Game's on. Want to watch?"

"Who's playing?"

"Braves and the Phillies."

Nick nodded and took a seat on the couch. The old man seemed to be holding up pretty well. He looked fit and trim and just as ornery as ever.

Gramps returned from the kitchen a few minutes later with two beers, a bag of chips, and something in a bowl.

"What's this?" Nick stared down at a beige dip flecked with bits of red peppers that smelled powerfully of cumin.

"Hummus. Have some. I made it."

"Okay." He *made* it? There was a time when Gramps's "making" something consisted of peeling off the plastic wrap and nuking it for six minutes. Nick took a reluctant taste. To his surprise, it was snappy with lot of bite. Just like Gramps.

They sat there in silence, watching the game. The Phillies were trampling the Braves and Gramps was not pleased. Nick knew well enough not to interrupt, but he couldn't concentrate on the stupid game.

Thoughts of Maddie rolled through his mind. They

should have finished what they'd begun in that camper because he couldn't think of much else besides getting her naked and sinking into her softness over and over. He wanted to lay her down on that pink chenille bedspread in her old room and do everything he should have done when he was eighteen.

From the time his grandfather wanted him to stay and commute to college, build up to manager in one of the local stores, Nick feared he'd too become a man with broken dreams, stuck selling shoes in the middle of Nowhereville. He wanted to become something, someone. He wanted out.

Don't get entangled with those Kingstons. You get that girl pregnant, and there'll be hell to pay. It could never work with someone like her. Rich girl and a poor boy. What are you thinking?

He'd broken her heart to protect her from a nothing life. Little did he know he'd broken his own as well.

Nick fidgeted on the lumpy couch, making a note on his phone to ship in a new one. And a new Laz-y-Boy, too.

"Old man, I need to talk to you."

"Yeah, what for?" His grandfather narrowed his brows, thicker, bushier versions of his own. He felt certain his grandfather had been a lady-killer in his own time, but somehow he'd ended up alone after Gran died all those years ago. Maybe Nick should find out why, or he'd end up the same way.

He stood and lifted the remote from the arm of his grandfather's chair.

"It's the top of the seventh," Gramps said with justifiable outrage.

"Geez, it's not the seventh game of the World Series.

I'll DVR it for you." Nick punched buttons, but Gramps grabbed the remote back and kept watching the game.

"That guy was out, I tell you. What a bad call. Let's see the instant replay. Told you that ump's an idiot."

Nick would just have to talk over the racket. He got up and paced. "Why won't you let me get you a better place to stay?"

Nick's grandfather kept one eye on the game. "I like this one just fine, thank you very much."

"I can buy you ten of these houses, you know that, don't you?" After the feud, Gramps had worked in the next town over but had stayed here to be close to Gran's aging parents. He'd never left Buckleberry Bend.

"Of course I do. But I like this house and besides, the new TV you bought me suits just fine. What's really bunching up your shorts?"

Nick breathed deeply. The old man could not show affection if he was threatened at gunpoint. He knew Gramps loved him. Yes, he knew. But just once he wanted to hear, *I'm proud of you, boy. You've done very well for yourself.* Instead, Gramps offered a stream of curt little phrases that could be taken a million different ways.

Nick had learned long ago not to expect any gushing. Gramps didn't do much ball-playing or PTA-attending, but he did encourage him to study and work hard. Even if they'd lived like two single guys in a bachelor pad, eating TV dinners and doing all the chores on an as-needed basis. But today he'd come for answers.

"I need to talk to you about the Kingston Shoe Company."

"Okay." Gramps's voice was flat but he looked like he'd

rather have his brand new TV taken away forever than talk about the past.

"It's in big trouble. The family is doing drastic things to save it." *Like selling their stocks to me.*

"Why are you telling me this? I washed my hands of all that business a long time ago."

"I want to know what happened."

"Things happened the way they did, and there's no undoing any of it." He pointed at the TV. "Oh, will you look at that? He walked another one!"

"Is it so horrible you can't even talk about it?"

"Sometimes people disappoint you, Nicky. Even the ones you trust the most. That's all I can say."

Nick looked at the man who raised him. He was tired of cryptic lines about never trusting anyone. He wanted answers, but Gramps was not a talker. Plus, the past was painful. For all of them.

"I'll get us another beer."

Nick wandered through the tiny linoleum-covered kitchen and into the garage to grab some beers from the extra fridge. A long pop-up table covered with charcoal and pastel drawings sat in the middle of the immaculately swept cement floor. Another table held strips of leather, ribbons, a variety of shoemaking tools, and wooden shoe lasts, some covered with material that made them look just like real shoes and that matched more drawings scattered nearby.

Nick sat down at a surprisingly expensive chair, one of those ergonomic models that probably cost several hundred dollars. The jerry-rigged lighting on top of the workspace was complex too. There was even a fancy electric heater, the kind he'd seen car mechanics use, suspended from the ceiling.

Drawing after drawing, shoe after shoe. Stilettos, flats, loafers. Complex engineering-quality drawings of soles and samples of funky materials to impact shock and affect balance. It was clear his granddad still hadn't given up on his dream. A dream he'd almost realized once. Just when he would have finally made it to New York…he'd gotten a five-year-old boy to raise. Gramps had made a good life for them. He'd provided everything a boy could need, and he never did make it back to New York. Now Nick wanted to give back.

"What's taking you so long?"

Nick looked up to see his grandfather standing in the doorway. He didn't want to make him uncomfortable, but he longed to be let in. "I got sidetracked." He picked up a stiletto, red and sleek, with an intricate flower embellishment. It was pretty, elegant, streamlined.

"This is a beautiful shoe," Nick said, hoping his grandfather would take the bait and discuss his work.

His grandfather walked over and fingered the tip. "Not just beautiful, Nicky. Easy on the feet, too."

"Maybe you should market it."

"Maybe I should."

"I have contacts in New York. I could help you—"

Gramps laughed softly. "I'm seventy-two years old. I think the gravy train has come and gone, son." He stacked some scattered papers and turned to go.

"I came here with Maddie Kingston for the weekend."

His grandfather turned back around. Those thick brows lifted again, but he didn't say a thing.

Now was Nick's chance to tell his granddad he was

buying the company so Gramps could have his final chance at success, at realizing his dream. But all Nick could see was Maddie silently trying to reassure her mother, that look of worried concern creasing a frown between her smooth brows as Derrick told him, *Thanks for coming to help Maddie with her crazy scheme.*

Except it wasn't so crazy. She was trying to bail out her family. Who could blame her for that? Nick opened the beat up fridge and grabbed two ice-cold beers, handed one to his granddad. It would be great to watch the rest of the game and forget about his problems.

"Sorry to hear about her father," his granddad said out of the blue.

Nick snapped to attention. Shut the fridge door. "What?"

"You don't know what happened?"

Nick must have looked as incredulous as he felt. A wave of nausea churned his stomach.

"Stroke," Gramps said. "Two months ago. Pretty severe. He's still at the rehab hospital."

Nick's heart tapped out a staccato rhythm that made it hard to hear. "Have you seen him?" A stroke? How could that be? He was only fifty-ish.

Puzzle pieces clicked into place. No wonder why Maddie quit her job…and planned to take charge of a company without any business experience under her belt.

Her dad was sick. *How sick?*

"Not my place to go," Gramps said.

Of course not. The feud. Nick wanted to tell his grandfather that was precisely why he should take the opportunity to go see Henry Kingston.

"Are you involved with her?" his grandfather asked.

Nick barely heard the question. "With Maddie? No. She…needed my advice. Now I understand why."

"You're offering business advice to them?"

"She's my friend, and she asked me, Gramps." Now Nick was the one who didn't want to talk.

"Well, the whole thing's unfortunate. I wish them well."

As Nick followed his grandfather back into the house, he wondered why the hell Maddie hadn't told him about her father. She'd taken a huge risk quitting her own job to take on this burden, without help. No one with a grain of business sense would ever have done it. The whole thing made him feel physically sick.

"We can order a pizza and watch your Phillies finish pummeling the Braves," Gramps said.

"Thanks, but I'd better be going."

Funny, but Nick left feeling like he was the one who'd just been pummeled.

Chapter Nine

It was nearly dark when Nick pulled into the Kingstons' driveway and punched his partner's number angrily into his phone. Did Preston not know the circumstances about Maddie's dad when they bought up those stocks?

No answer. Nick pinched the bridge of his nose. Equal parts fury and sadness ripped through him in waves. His relationship with Maddie had eroded to the point where she couldn't even tell him the truth, and he knew he was to blame. But he couldn't understand why her family would allow her to shoulder this Herculean task alone. They'd taken advantage of her kind, self-effacing nature.

All his pleasure at finally settling the score between their families faded as quickly as twilight's last light. He never regretted a business decision, but this was a game changer. How the hell could he dismantle a company when Maddie's dad was sick and disabled?

Every cell in his body knew the answer. *He couldn't.* But

he had to.

The family was outside roasting marshmallows. He searched the flickering faces around the fire. No Maddie. Nick tried to act laid back and calm as he hugged Cat and shook hands with her fiancé, Robert. Mrs. Kingston moved over on the outdoor couch and offered him a seat and a skewer.

"Want a marshmallow, Holter?" Derrick asked like he was really challenging him to a duel. Jenna rolled her eyes, making Nick wonder if being tight-assed was this guy's usual state of being.

"No, thanks. Actually, I was wondering if anyone knows where Maddie is?"

Derrick, Jenna, and Maddie's mom shrugged, but Cat just stared into the fire.

Judging by the times Maddie mentioned her sister on the long car ride, they were close. "Can I speak to you in private?" Nick asked.

"Sure." Nervously tucking her hair behind her ears, she got up and followed Nick to the driveway, where they stood out of earshot of the others.

"Tell me where she is."

"Well, it's nice to see you, too. How long's it been? Ten years?"

"Congrats on your engagement. Where's Maddie?"

"I don't know."

Nick paced, his loafers crunching on the gravel driveway. He ticked off items on his fingers. "I've checked the hospital parking lot, the rehab center, drove through downtown, and stopped at the park. I need to talk to her."

Cat lowered her voice. "Look, I'm the only one who

knows about the auction and the shares. I'm sorry if you have things to discuss with my sister. But if she doesn't want to get found, I'm not ratting her out."

Clearly stubbornness ran in the bloodlines of this family. But Kingston Shoes was no longer just a mismanaged company circling the toilet bowl. It was a *family* in crisis. Somehow, he'd managed to land smack dab in the middle.

"Please." He was incapable of begging. This was as far as he could go.

Cat crossed her arms. "Why should I?"

Well, maybe he'd have to go a little further.

"She never told me about your father. I had no idea."

"She didn't want to tell you. She didn't *trust* you enough to tell you."

Her words stabbed like dagger pricks. Nick had grown up not trusting. He'd heard it over and over from his grandfather that trusting leads to getting screwed. Yet he always thought of himself as a person *others* could trust to be honest, work hard, and do the right thing.

The fact that Maddie didn't, hurt him. A lot.

"You may not believe this, but I haven't got a penchant for revenge up my sleeve. I am sorry about what happened to your dad."

Cat sighed. "Honestly, I don't know if you're a friend or an enemy. But if you want to find her, you might try the dock."

"Thanks." That's all Nick needed to take off at a jog down the sloping yard to where it ended in a wall of woods. It was fully dark now, and he wasn't sure he'd be able to find the path he remembered that led to the lake.

The air still held its humid heaviness, but it was pleasant

in that hot-summer-night kind of way, with bullfrogs *blurping* and crickets *skreeing* and the spilled-puddle Milky Way in full view above the treetops. It reminded him of being young and carefree but also brought into bitter contrast how much had changed. When was the last time he'd taken a few moments to enjoy nature? Or have someone to enjoy it with?

Instinct served him well because he found the path using his cell phone light, and a minute later parted his way through the brush to a clear view of the lake. Maddie sat on the far end of the dock, her knees bent up, head bent low and her arms encircled around her calves. A muffled sniff sounded over the frog melodies.

A sickening feeling swirled in his stomach. Any kind of crying made him feel helpless and vulnerable, two things he'd vowed never to be. When women cried, he usually ran far and away.

Nick should be thrilled that all this chaos made the company an easy target for a quick kill, but he knew he couldn't bring himself to feel that way. Maddie needed a friend. With all his heart, he wanted to be that friend. Yet he'd run from her last year without so much as a word after Gramps had ended up in the hospital for a heart scare, managing to tell himself his loyalty to his grandfather was everything.

He was incapable of trusting anyone enough to let go all the way. He'd never had a long-term relationship. Some of that might have been his grandfather ranting for much of his childhood over his hurt of being cut out of the business. But maybe it went a lot deeper.

After his parents and sister died, he'd been afraid to love anyone for fear of suffering like that again. The business world was more predictable and a whole lot less emotionally risky. It made sense to him to thrust everything he had into becoming a success.

Trouble was, he had no idea how to do anything else.

He cleared his throat. "Maddie," he said. His voice sounded stiff and raw and an octave too nervous.

Her head bobbed up like a buoy in a boat's wake, and she quickly swiped her hands over her cheeks. She gave a half-hearted wave but kept facing the lake.

He walked along the old dock, feeling the slight bounce from his weight and the low rumble of his leather soles on the weathered old wood. The same mossy, fishy scent accosted him, stirring a fleet of old memories.

Everyone in Buckleberry grew up surrounded by Lake Watchacatchee. On weekends it was loaded with pontoon boats and families that headed out for a day cruising around and fishing and swimming. There were cabins to rent and a lodge and restaurant where people could eat overlooking the water.

The lake was tied to all the important moments in his life. Learning to swim. Endless summer picnics and barbecues. His first job at the lakefront restaurant. Necking with girls on the backroads near the marshlands. And almost making love to Maddie in an old canoe not far from this dock. They'd taken a picnic out and watched the sun set. The moon was full and the lake so calm it looked like black glass. She'd been young and inexperienced, and he'd made her come. He still remembered the look on her face as she let go for the first time—a beautiful prism of feelings, pleasure as the waves hit her and she rode them through, then shock and surprise. And so much more. Her eyes softened with feelings he couldn't even name, and she'd reached for him, eager and willing to please him as well.

But he didn't deserve her. She was too good, too loving, and he'd had no business doing that with her. The boy from across the tracks, shunned by the town and her family. Impossible. So he broke it off.

In the past, Nick had failed her in every way possible. But by God, he wanted to help her now.

He didn't say a word, just lowered himself next to Maddie. To his surprise, she clutched a fishing pole. She'd tied her hair back in a ponytail, reminding him of the vulnerable girl she once was. They'd sat on this dock before, dreaming of the future, making plans for college and the big lives they'd lead.

"Catch anything?" he asked.

"Not yet." Her tone was quiet and a little optimistic, like it was the most normal thing in the world to be dangling a fishing pole off the dock after dark on a starry July night.

He nodded and leaned back on his hands. The dock was still pleasantly warm from the sun beating down all day, and he had a sudden urge to sprawl his tired body out and just lie there and stare up at the stars. And then drag Maddie down with him. Plant deep, thorough kisses on her soft lips and her neck, slide his hands from the smooth skin of her waist up under her shirt, and take both of them to that dangerous edge where all these problems did not exist.

"Have you *ever* caught anything out here?" He squinted across the quiet surface of the lake.

"Haven't caught anything for years."

"So why the sudden interest in fishing?" He recalled her fear of impaling worms and minnows. She'd never had the heart.

Maddie looked at him. In the moonlight, drying streaks tracked down her cheeks. Something deep inside his guts snapped like an old guitar string. He felt helpless. All he could do was stare back into those big, worried eyes.

Reason and sense fought with an overpowering urge to tug her into his arms and make it all better. He was inches away from her, close enough to smell her clean, citrusy scent and see the twinkle of imitation diamond studs in her ears.

He fought against the tide of emotion like a man buried under a wall of water, clutching his way to the surface. He didn't *want* feelings to get in the way of this weekend. He didn't *want* to cloud his head when he had to make tough choices that impacted so many people. That affected his grandfather, his partner, Maddie, and her family.

On impulse, Nick reached for her, but just then the fishing line lurched. Maddie grabbed for the pole, which bumped and rattled down the dock. Nick sat up and caught it just before it was dragged off the dock. The pole bent, the line pulling it down in big, impressive tugs.

"What kind of bait did you use?" Nick asked incredulously. They were standing now, all their attention on the commotion in the water.

"I-I wasn't even fishing. I just grabbed the pole. I think one of the boys left it down here before dinner."

Nick couldn't help smiling. Just like her to not want to show any weakness. He handed her the pole. "Nothing to do but reel it in."

Maddie stood up and pulled up on the pole. She cranked until something shot out of the water—a little something, about eight inches long, flashing silver in the moonlight.

"Oh my God, it's a fish!"

Nick laughed. "Maybe you shouldn't go fishing if you don't like the consequences."

"It's so little. The way the line was pulling, I expected…"

"What? Shamu?" Nick reached out and grabbed the line. Flipping and flopping on the end was a small but flashy fish, its silver scales glinting in the moonlight. "It's a sunfish." He flashed his light on the flailing creature. "The red-breasted kind."

Maddie did a weird little dance around the dock, prancing about and flapping her hands. "Put the poor thing back, Nick. Please."

"Don't freak out. It's just a little fish." Her usual tough demeanor had all but crumbled. This was one hundred percent girlie behavior, and if she weren't so earnest, he'd burst out laughing.

"I don't want to kill him." Her eyes pleaded, so he grabbed hold of the fish. The hook protruded from its jaw. Its gills were heaving and its mouth gasping and its big eye was looking at him in what he imagined was distress. Maddie turned away and covered her face with her hands. "I can't look. Tell me when it's over."

Nick twisted the hook out as gently as he could. "Sure you don't want to fry him up for breakfast?" He bit back a smile.

"Let. It. Go."

"All right then. If you're sure." Nick tossed it back into the water where it hit with a satisfied plop.

Maddie exhaled loudly. Nick roared with laughter. "You come across as being so tough, but here's a little eight-inch fish doing you in."

"I'm not tough." She stood there on the dock with her arms crossed, looking mock-offended, the moonlight shining off the highlights in her hair and giving her a fairy tale cast. He fought the overwhelming urge to kiss her. "At least not as tough as you," she said. "You definitely don't strike me as a catch-and-release kind of guy."

So, she perceived him a grab-and-never-let-go kind? "Why is that?"

"Oh, just that you've built an empire grabbing on to opportunities one at a time."

"You make me sound greedy. Maybe I'm just ambitious."

"I'm sure that sometimes that's a very blurred distinction."

"Yeah, but sometimes you've got to let the little ones go." Nick stepped closer and fingered an errant curl. "And you are tough, but maybe it's okay to show people you're vulnerable once in a while."

"I can't afford to do that."

"You can with me." He took a deep breath and plunged. "I know about your dad."

Her face twisted up, a patchwork of pain and misery.

In one movement, he dropped the pole and pulled her to him. She tensed in his arms, but he tightened his hold, wrapped his arms full around her and tucked her head under his chin until at last she relaxed a bit. God, he loved the way she smelled, fruity and fresh and she was just so damn pretty. He wanted to let loose and plow his hands through those soft luscious curls, pull her head back and drag his lips to hers, use his body to comfort and possess her and make her forget every last blessed pain. Replace all logical thought with hot, pure sex.

They'd used sex instead of communication in the past,

and it had turned out disastrously. For once he needed to think of what she needed. And right now that was a friend.

She was still trigger-ready tense, every muscle cocked and loaded like a slingshot ready to fly. "I visited my dad tonight. He's still so weak. I expected him to be like I always knew him—just—Dad. But he's not. Everything's different."

"It's okay to be afraid."

She pulled back a little and looked at him. "I shouldn't have told you that. I'm fine and I—I've got to go. Thanks for saving the fish." She slipped out of his arms and ran up the dock.

"Maddie, wait!"

For the first time he wondered if the company was worth the price both their families had paid. If only it were as easy to toss out the past as it was to throw that fish back into the water. But when their grandfathers parted ways, they left behind a disaster zone of twisted feelings, a train wreck of anger and bitterness.

How to ever rebuild, start anew? Would it ever be possible if he followed through with his plan to install Gramps as new head of a new company?

Nick caught up to her just outside the strip of woods. He didn't bother asking why she didn't tell him the truth. A company without a head was an easy target for takeover. Plus she had no reason to trust him. He stopped her with his words.

"Have you told him what's happening to the company?" The sinking feeling he had in his stomach already told him the answer.

Maddie spun to face him. "Dad needs to focus everything on his recovery. It would kill him to know the company is going under. Just kill him."

"Nothing you do can stop what's already happened. The company's been in trouble for a long time. He deserves to know."

Guilt pricked at him. Didn't she deserve to know he owned the majority of shares in Kingston Shoes? But how could he tell her now?

Her eyes flashed with grim determination. "I know I can turn it around. I'm going back to the drawing board about product and design. I *can* make a difference." She squeezed her eyes shut as if debating whether or not to say more. "I know you don't see how important this is, but Kingston Shoes is seventy years old. That name is my family's legacy. I have to find a way to save it."

Her chin tilted up at a resolute angle. Every instinct warned him not to let her get to him. She was too proud to beg but Nick understood what she wanted. So he chose his words carefully. "I can tour the company and give you my best assessment on the options, if you want."

"You're not going to dismantle us?"

Oh, hell. Of course he wasn't. But he couldn't give up on helping his grandfather. So exactly what was he promising her? He wasn't sure.

Hairs pricked on the back of Nick's neck. Seconds ticked as he weighed his options, bad and worse. Finally he answered. "No, I'm not going to dismantle the company."

She jumped up and kissed him on the cheek. Just a peck. She was grateful and relieved and that made him inexplicably happy.

He held her lightly at the waist, and every instinct made him want to tighten his hold, but he made himself pull away.

"Thank you." She paused. "I still don't understand why you want the company so badly. If it's to make up for how your grandfather was treated years ago, maybe I can arrange some recompense…"

"It's not about money, Maddie. My grandfather got stuck spending his life managing a chain of poorly performing shoe stores and raising me. I saw an opportunity to give him the chance he never got."

"So exactly what is it you want?"

"My grandfather had big dreams that he couldn't achieve because he had to raise me. I'm in a position to help him achieve those dreams."

"So you want us to give him a job?"

Nick shrugged. He wasn't about to tell her the job he was planning just happened to be that of CEO. "I'll know more after my analysis."

She searched his face before answering. "Okay. I accept your word."

"Great." They'd finally agreed on something. But still he felt he owed her more. "Maddie, I'm sorry about last night, in the camper."

She frowned. "Sorry about what?"

"About, you know. Almost having sex."

She let that settle before answering. "Oh."

"What I'm saying is, I want us to be friends."

Her brows lifted in surprise. "You want us to be friends?"

Maybe he'd just tossed his common sense in the water with that fish. "Yeah. Seems like you need one about now. You okay with that?"

"Um, yeah. Sure. Thanks."

He guided her through the bramble with a light touch

on her back but otherwise kept his hands to himself.

Friends. It was the right thing to do. He'd use his contacts and influence however he could to help her and her family while keeping his grandfather's interests at heart. Keep it casual and businesslike and his emotions out of it, because he wasn't capable of offering her anything more.

Chapter Ten

"It's a perfect day for the festival," Maddie said as Nick left the house with her the next morning. She carried one of her mother's famous mixed berry pies and handed Nick the other. Maddie had promised to deliver them to Ophelia Gorsky, the town librarian and one of her mother's oldest friends, who also happened to be supervising the pie contest.

"Let's not discuss business today," Maddie said. "Call a truce. Just enjoy the festival."

"There'll be plenty of time for business tomorrow," Nick said, eyeing her from the side. She wore a red tank top that showed off her nice rack and a jean skirt that showed off her great legs. Tiny American flags dangled from her ears. To anyone else on the street she probably looked apple-pie fresh and clean, but to Nick she looked downright dangerous. She had no idea how badly he wanted to ditch the pies and the festival and drag her off caveman-style to somewhere quiet and private.

"Oh, I almost forgot." She shifted the pie and pulled something narrow and flat out of her skirt pocket. "Hold out your wrist."

He frowned, but she laughed and made him surrender his hand as she tied a red, white, and blue braided thread bracelet around his wrist. "Logan and Alex made it for you. With my help."

He eyed her suspiciously. "Why…why'd they do that?"

She knotted the bracelet. "Um, because for some reason they like you."

"Oh." Nick had never had much interaction with children, and the fact that he'd made some kind of impression on two little kids just by chasing them and being silly floored him. He jiggled his wrist, inordinately pleased with the simple gift that dangled next to his flashy watch. "I reckon this is more fashionable for the Fourth, anyway."

"Looks great with your Rolex, too." Maddie grinned and looked him over. "You look nice and casual today."

He was happy she'd noticed he'd tried to loosen up a little, wearing a plain gray t-shirt and cargo shorts and ditching his penny loafers for flip-flops.

As they walked the five blocks to downtown, Nick fielded calls and returned texts. It wasn't easy, because Maddie was always exclaiming about something. "Look at those gorgeous petunias hanging from the lampposts!" or "Everybody's gathering to talk outside of Ida's Pancakes," or "I heard they're having gourmet food trucks this year for the first time." While his own stomach churned with bad vibes as they walked along the bumpy sidewalks of the old town, he could sense her excitement at being back in a place she loved.

"If you're so busy with work all the time, how is it you have a tan?" Maddie asked as Nick finished a call.

He answered without looking up from his phone. "You can return calls from a great outdoor location just as well as from a stuffy air conditioned office."

"Does that great outdoor location happen to be your Caribbean island?"

He dismissed her comment with a chuckle. She already thought he was a snob, no need to elaborate right now.

"You always did love outdoor sports. Hiking, rock climbing, skiing. Do you really skydive?"

He stopped walking. "You've asked me that before. Why don't you believe that I skydive?"

"Well, you're complicated. You've always loved order and control. Your love of risk surprises me."

His gaze flicked slowly over her bare legs, shorts, and tank top, and lingered on her boobs. She blushed under his very male scrutiny. "Oh, I very much enjoy taking some risks." He'd had to in order to become as successful as he had. "But to answer your question, I prefer tamer sports now."

"Like what?" she asked, clearly trying to steer the discussion to safer ground.

"Oh, you know…cliff diving, train surfing."

"Train surfing?" She covered her eyes in horror. "No, don't tell me. I don't want to know."

He pulled her hand from her face and made her look at him. He gazed into the most spectacular sky blue eyes he'd ever seen. "I'm just messing with you. I might like adventure, but I'm not crazy."

A mischievous look glinted in those eyes. "If you're done with your phone, can I use it?"

"I think I've made all the calls I need for now. Here you go." He handed over the phone. Maddie promptly tossed it into the official riveted blue mailbox that sat on the pavement in front of the stately brick post office.

"Hey! Why'd you go and do that?" Nick's tone held a mixture of disbelief and outrage.

"Because you promised no business today."

"I meant *your* business. Not mine." He set his pie down on one of the post office window ledges, opened the mailbox door, and peered into the dark void.

"It's just nice to be one hundred percent present, is all," she said.

"Yeah, well, right now I'm one hundred percent pissed." He bent down and snaked his arm inside, grasping nothing but air and nearly getting his shoulder wedged in the narrow space.

"You'd better not get caught tampering with that. It's a federal crime."

He shot her a murderous look.

"I'll get Mr. Jameson to unlock it first thing Monday morning." She did not sound contrite.

"Monday morning? That's two full days away." His voice sounded high and overwrought. Well, he was, damn it. She was more than capable of getting him all worked up, shuffling his perfectly ordered life, which was her plan, of course. He was certain she wanted his undivided attention on the good townspeople of Buckleberry Bend so he could be fully aware of how his decisions would impact all her friends and neighbors.

"You can borrow mine for any emergencies," she said.

"I'm going to get you back for this. Mark my words."

She shrugged then squinted into the sun. "Want to go check out the booths?"

"Now that I'm done with work for the day," he said wryly, "I'd love to."

They strolled through the park to a long row of artisan booths. Pritchett Park was crow-*ded*, everyone out on the lazy summer day, meandering around the oaks and manicured gardens for the town's largest annual event.

They passed the bronze statue of General Krandall Pervis Pritchett, Buckleberry Bend's first mayor, which faced north like every proper Southern general. The statue was bedecked with a leafy crown, flower ropes of daisies, and a large sign announcing the 5K race, the barbequed rib burn-off, the pie judging, and the berry-themed dinner to be held at the lakefront restaurant.

Maddie waved and called out to people as they passed. Seemed like she knew everyone and always had a kind word to say, inquiring after their relatives, sympathizing with their troubles. And they clearly liked her, wished her father well. She fit in here as tightly as the last piece in a jigsaw puzzle.

Everyone milled about the booths, looking for fun and a chance to see berries baked, mashed, put into sauces and syrups, wine, soup, muffins, breads, jams, pies, face masks, and candles.

Nick hadn't recognized anyone so far and that was fine with him. He just wanted to survive this day and do what he came to do. That meant focusing on his goal of helping his granddad and figuring out some way to help Maddie's family. And not getting too caught up in everyone's troubles.

After all, he wasn't the one who ran the shoe company into the ground. If anything, his money would save it. But not in the way Maddie would want.

Another reason he couldn't have her. He couldn't give her the solution she wanted, to keep her family in charge. Not after what they'd done to his grandfather.

"You're not happy to be back home?" she asked.

He released a pent-up sigh. "You're the one with the big happy family."

Maddie halted and stared. "My father's sick, our business is falling apart, and I have the grandmother from hell. Not to mention a brother who verbally strong-arms me like I'm one of his Army recruits. Big happy family we are *not*."

"At least you have a family. You put down roots here."

"The fact that you're so successful today is a testament to your inner strength. You should be proud of your accomplishments. You're very well respected in your field."

He snorted. "People are always friendly when they know you've got money."

"Remember that dance?" Maddie changed the subject as they passed a guitar player crooning a country tune.

"What dance?"

"The fall one where you came with Ashby Wilkerson." The most popular girl in school. But he'd ended up noticing Maddie.

They hadn't really seen each other since kindergarten, just here and there, where they threw each other hasty glances and quickly looked away. Nick knew he should stay away from her, pretty as a princess, all cheery and unspoiled by darkness. Yet Maddie kept drawing him back to her with the intensity of a rip current.

"I saw you leave the gym, and I told my date I had to go to the bathroom," Maddie said.

He *tsked*. "Shameless hussy. Pursuing me like that."

"When I got outside, there you were, leaning against the building, looking dark and dangerous. I think you were smoking."

"I had a hunch you'd come out looking for me. So I ran ahead and pretended I went out to take a smoke. I was trying to act badass."

"You never told me that."

"I never told you a lot of things."

"Like what?"

"Like I thought you were the most beautiful girl I'd ever seen."

Maddie shook her head as if to fend off the comment, which had probably crossed the just-friends line. But Nick didn't want her to shake it off. He wanted her to remember.

"We both had dates," Nick said, "so I asked you to meet me that Sunday at the Pumpkin Fest. Remember the Kissing Booth?"

She laughed. "How could I forget? I paid you a dollar for a kiss."

"For *that* kiss, you should've paid me two."

"I wrote my phone number on the dollar."

Nick shook his head and grinned. "Shameless again."

"Do you still smoke?" she asked.

"Gave that bad habit up a long time ago."

"Guess I was a habit you gave up, too." Maddie bit her lower lip and looked away.

Oh, hell. He'd broken up with her and then took Ashby on a couple dates to cement the breakup, to send the message there would be no getting back together. God, he'd been an asshole.

"Maddie, I—"

Just then, May Felding, an old friend from high school, smiled and waved at them from her organic cosmetics booth.

"Let's go say hey." Maddie ran off a little too eagerly.

Nick took up her hand and clutched it tightly so she couldn't pull away without making a scene.

"Let go." She glared at him. "We're not dating. That was over a long time ago. I'm sorry I brought it up."

"Walk with me, Maddie." He placed his other hand on top of their joined hands and beseeched. "Enjoy the afternoon with me. Remember the truce?"

"Fine," she said darkly. "I'll keep the truce but that does *not* mean I have to hold your hand."

They'd only gone a few steps when Ophelia Gorsky spun around from looking at a display of glazed pottery, setting the peacock feathers atop her blue straw hat bobbing.

"Well, I do declare. Seeing you two together again after all this time. Life sure is funny sometimes." She glanced from Nick to Maddie. "And might those be your mama's famous pies?"

"Yes, ma'am," Maddie said as Mrs. Gorsky took her pie, set it down on one of May's tables, and gave her a hug.

"Your poor mama's been baking up a storm ever since your daddy got sick. It's her therapy, isn't it?" She took the pie from Nick, then she enveloped him in a hug too. He stiffened in surprise but recovered enough to awkwardly return it to one of the only people who had never held his background against him.

If Mrs. Gorsky noticed Nick's discomfort, it didn't faze her. "She needs it, since your grandmother's been hanging around the house so much lately. Nicholas, I'm so very proud of you. Hear you're a big businessman now. All those library books you checked out did some good."

"You always ordered me the ones our library didn't have, Mrs. G."

"Goodness, all those adventure books. Explorers' journals, spies, pirates. Laurence of Arabia, Robert Louis Stevenson…"

"You read all those?" Maddie quirked a brow.

Nick never blushed, but dammed if he felt his face heat up.

Mrs. Gorsky wagged a finger at Maddie. "Unlike you, Miss I'll-sneak-the-Kathleen-Woodiwiss-and-Barbara-Cartland-books-out-before-anyone-catches-me. Oh, dear, I almost forgot, Mr. Hummertz is sick today, and we need another judge. Nicholas, would you do us the honor?"

"Thanks anyway, but my taste buds aren't exactly discerning enough for—"

"Nonsense. All you need is a hearty appetite for pie and the bravery to give your own opinion. I'm certain you'll do a fine job."

Nick would rather have kept a low profile. Besides, he was more a cake person. But Mrs. Gorsky had always been kind to him, and he found himself agreeing to show up at the pie booth in a half hour.

They moved on to May's booth just as she scooped up a mischievous looking toddler who was sucking on a tube of berry-flavored lip gloss. "Beauregard Mason Felding," she said, "don't you dare open any more of those. Is that clear?"

May bounced the toddler on her hip as she hugged Maddie and Nick. "That's his third one. Good thing they're nontoxic. I always did think y'all were such a cute couple. Glad to see you together."

Maddie ignored that and spoke to May while she perused the varieties of organic soaps and samples of blueberry exfoliating face mask. "How's Beau Senior?"

Nick remembered Beau and Maddie had started together at the shoe store, working the floor, sizing people's feet,
and lugging boxes in and out of the storeroom all day long
for customers. Now he managed the main store.

"He's just taken on the Chesterland store too," May
said. "But he's worried—we're all worried, especially with
the baby coming." She paused to rub a small baby bump.
"And we have two more at home—" She pulled a bar of
organic soap out of little Beau's grasp.

"Oh, May." Maddie bit her lower lip. Nick knew she
wanted to offer reassurance but had none to give.

"That's why I've been trying to get my own business up
and running, you know, just in case."

"Well, everything looks really yummy. I'd love to try the
face mask and what else would you recommend?" If she
couldn't save May's husband's job, she could at least buy out
all her products. Just like Maddie.

"Everything is organic. My favorite is the lemon verbena
soap. Here, smell a sample. The strawberry is really good
too."

"I don't know, Nick. Which do you like?" Maddie picked
up the samples and waved them under Nick's nose.

"Here, Sweetheart. Let's get both." Before she could
protest, he'd pulled out his wallet and bought both kinds,
plus matching shampoo, conditioner, and body lotion. He
hugged May good-bye and even patted her little boy on the
head.

As if buying body care products would scrub away

any guilt he might feel from whatever happened to these people's jobs once he took charge. He reminded himself the company was in big trouble long before he bought his shares. But wasn't he responsible in some big way now that he controlled its fate?

"You didn't have to buy all that," Maddie said as they steered their way into the food vendor aisle.

"Organic berry products are my weakness," he said. "All that shopping gave me an appetite. You hungry?"

"I'm always hungry for barbecue."

They approached a vending truck where meat was being smoked and slow cooked over an open flame.

"Hey, Clay," Maddie said as they approached the truck. A well-built man in a muscle shirt and with a large tattoo on his arm left the food truck and ran outside, immediately lifting her up and swinging her around.

Whoa. Talk about an overly exuberant welcome from Muscle Man.

"You didn't tell me you were coming this weekend. I had to hear it from my grandma talking to your grandma," he said.

"It was a last-minute decision."

"Well, I know you've got what it takes to get that shoe company up and running."

The guy was still touching her and making moon eyes, and Nick didn't like it one bit.

"Nick, you remember Clayton Wilbanks?" Maddie asked. "He attended cooking school in New York, and now he's head chef at The Lodge."

Nick shook his old classmate's hand. The Lodge was the best restaurant in town, set up on a hill with a beautiful view of Lake Watchacatchee. "Heard your place is doing very well. Congratulations."

"Talk about town is you're doing pretty well yourself. You're here to troubleshoot what's going on at Kingston Shoes?"

"Yes." That was the story they'd agreed on telling. Funny that now it just happened to be true.

"I wouldn't want you poking your nose anywhere it doesn't belong, though."

Nick stiffened at his sudden change in tone. "Maddie invited me here, Clay."

"I'm sure she did, because Maddie is a kind and trusting person. But she's been through enough. Especially with bad men who masquerade as do-gooders."

"Clay, please," Maddie said. "I can take care of myself."

Nick pointed to the grill as he gave Clay the stink-eye. "Maybe you'd better pay attention because I think you're burning your barbecue."

Clay, startled, went to check his meat. Then he got back in Nick's face. "You don't strike me as a do-gooder, either, from what I've been reading about you. Different woman and a different company take-over every week."

"Clay!" Maddie looked horrified.

Clay telegraphed a look at Maddie that was half loyalty and half desperation. Man, he had it bad. Nick actually felt sorry for him.

"I can't help it," Clay said. "I can't sit by and allow you to think this guy finally has your best interests at heart. He certainly didn't when he left you high and dry in high school."

"He does have our best interests at heart. He's trying to help us find solutions." Maddie sounded sincere. Guilt hammered at Nick's conscience. He *wanted* it to be true. If only he could find a way to pull this company out of the trenches and find a way to help his grandfather, too. But the odds of making both families happy were about one in a zillion.

"My father's worked for Kingston Shoes for twenty-eight years." Clay gestured with his grill fork into the distance. "And I can point to at least ten other families in shouting distance who can say the same. All I know is, Mr. Holter, you'd better not make promises you can't keep."

"I'm not going to lie, Clay. The company is in trouble, but I promised Maddie my best assessment."

Clay finally prepared their barbecue and they took it to a far picnic table, out of sight of Clay's truck. Nick sat and stole a sip of Maddie's fresh-squeezed lemonade just as he'd done countless times before. "Sir Gallahad was ready to plant me a facer. Hope that was really hot sauce he put on my sandwich and not arsenic."

Maddie laughed. "Clay's just looking out for me."

Nick didn't reach for his food, even though he'd recently quipped that the sweet, melt-in-your-mouth barbecue was probably the only thing he missed about this place.

"He married?"

Maddie took a bite of her sandwich. "No."

"Dating someone?"

Maddie frowned.

"He's got his sights fixed on you, Maddie."

"You're wrong. He's been a good friend since you and I broke up in high school."

"Well, I know a look in a man's eye and let me tell you, he wants to date you. Bad."

"Are you *jealous*?" She'd said it to be funny but—wait—had she really? He *was* acting jealous. And this whole weird afternoon was feeling a lot like the thing he'd wanted to avoid the most: a date. The easy camaraderie, the jokes, the strolling along, the reminiscing…

Nick stared into Maddie's summer blue eyes. Would she still want to hear the word *yes* after all these years? How could he still want to say it?

"Damn right I am." Nick watched Maddie's sweet face blush. What was he doing? *Shit.* He'd totally lost sight of his goal of friendship, so he backpedaled. "I mean, who wouldn't be jealous of someone who makes barbecue as good as this?"

The expectant look fell into a heavy frown.

Even after all these years, he was still an expert at pushing her away.

That stupid answer would have been enough to shut the old Maddie down.

Instead, she set down her barbecue, wiped the napkin carefully over her mouth. "That answer's not good enough. I want to know the straight truth. Are you jealous of Clay?"

The food churned in Nick's stomach. Despite the fun they'd been having, it was best to put up the same mask as always to hide his real feelings. He set down his own sandwich, took off his sunglasses, and sighed, preparing to toss out another sarcastic quip. He looked into her eyes, so resolute, so demanding of the simple truth.

The quip melted on his lips. "You're damn right I'm jealous." Her expression turned to shock, but she couldn't have been more surprised than he was. He'd be damned if he'd sit here and allow her to end up with Clayton Wilbanks, the guy who followed her around like a puppy dog in high school. He wasn't the man she needed any more than the rodeo guy was. *Not at all.*

The hell with being friends. That had lasted all of an hour and he was tired of denying the truth. At that moment, he didn't care about the impossibility of being able to save her company and satisfy his grandfather at the same time. "It's not over, Maddie. It's still not over between us. We need to talk."

Chapter Eleven

Nick stood and walked around to her side of the picnic table. He pulled Maddie up, his strong hands gripping her at the elbows. She had to place her hand against his rock solid chest to prevent herself from bumping into him.

Their gazes caught and held. "I thought we were just going to be friends," she said, a little out of breath.

He eyed her hungrily. "Not working for me. Let's go somewhere where we can discuss this."

She'd barely said okay when a high-pitched woman's voice sounded behind them.

"Madison Kingston, you aren't still dressing mannequins at Macy's, are you?"

Oh, God, no. Not Ashby Wilkerson, socialite of Buckleberry Bend, former bitch extraordinaire. The girl Nick dated after he'd broken up with Maddie after prom.

Be nice, an inner voice warned. *Maybe she's changed.*

Yeah, right. And the rocks at Stonehenge recently moved.

"Well, hello, Ashby. How nice to see you again." Maddie dragged her gaze away from Nick. Her jaw ached from the wide, stiff smile she forced.

"Hello, Madison. Nicholas." Ashby's gaze lingered on Nick, taking a long, slow look from his muscular legs to his narrow waist and his broad chest, up to the chiseled features of his face.

Alarm bells rang inside Maddie's head. It was just her sense of a predator nearby, one with a long, mean history, but surely all that was in the past?

Nick made polite conversation. Maddie couldn't read his expression from behind the dark glasses he'd put back on. Ashby still looked as peaches-and-cream beautiful as always, from her sun-streaked blond hair and lovely aqua eyes to her floral-patterned silk dress, high heels, and pearls, probably the same set she'd gotten for her Sweet Sixteen. She looked like she was on the way to afternoon tea with the girls, circa 1962.

Ashby had been chasing after Nick for as long as memories had been recorded on paper. Ever since that dance when Nick had chosen Maddie over her, the woman had tried everything in her power to wreak havoc on their relationship. And she'd finally succeeded after Nick broke up with Maddie. Of course, she'd ended up marrying the high school quarterback, but they'd recently divorced, which probably explained why she was on the prowl.

Mrs. Gorsky beckoned to Nick from the pie tent, and he took his leave. As soon as he was out of earshot, Ashby took the opportunity to show her true personality. "So, Madison, did the dummy dressing job in Philly not work out, dear?"

"I reckon it was just a tad too complex for the likes of

little ol' me." Maddie fanned herself by flapping her hands near her face, distressed-Southern-belle fashion.

"Or maybe you're looking to marry another jobless cowboy?"

Maddie gasped. No, she would not succumb to immature, irrational behavior. Just because Ashby made every single hair on her body stand up on end and riled every fight-or-flight instinct she had—in the direction of *fight*.

Maddie strained to think of an insult, but she came up empty. Ashby lived in a two hundred-year-old antebellum mansion stuffed full of antiques and her grandma's fancy bone china, and sat on the board of every women's group in town. She had beauty, brains, and popularity, so there wasn't much to insult except her bone-deep meanness.

Maddie could cut deep and bring up her divorce, but she'd never punch someone where it really hurt. Well, unless her life was threatened. Did stealing Nick, who wasn't even hers anymore, count as a life threat?

Ashby geared up to take another cheap shot. "You'd much rather come home and muck up your daddy's company, now, wouldn't you? God help the good citizens of Buckleberry Bend."

Maddie breathed deeply. She was in control. She was mature and calm, and she would prove she had better defenses than in high school. "That's what I'm trying to do, Ashby. Help all those good citizens keep their jobs. Now, why don't you go taste a pie or something?"

"Actually, I'm in charge of organizing the pie booth for Ophelia, and I came to explain the judging to Nick."

Ashby walked off to the pie tent, but a Category Five hurricane could not stop Maddie from following. When Nick

met with the other judges, Maddie stood behind him looking at the spread of beautiful pies set out and catalogued
on cloth-covered rectangular tables. Ashby pointed out her
own two pies, strawberry and blueberry, then went to direct
the pie ladies, mostly her posse from high school who still
followed in her shadow. On the way, she whispered in Maddie's ear, "I want you to stay away from Nick."

Really? Did she think they were still in high school? "I
think Nick can make his own choices, Ashby." *And so can I.*

"I slept with him on prom night, you know. After he
broke up with you."

Maddie closed her eyes. Funny how Ashby could insult
her poor romantic choices, her previous bad jobs, and her
choice to come back and run her father's company without
raising her basest impulses. But one mention of Nick, and
Maddie wanted to wrestle, cat fight, and yank her perfect
hair.

Maddie pictured herself, the smile still pasted on her face.
She was nice little Maddie Kingston, everybody's friend. She
didn't rock the boat, and she did her best to please everybody, regardless of what that meant for her.

Well, she wasn't going to take it anymore. Starting right
now.

"Maybe you did, Ashby, but that was ancient history.
Nick won't warm your bed tonight because he'll be in mine."
Shock and fury raged through her like a dangerous, swollen
river. Nice girl Maddie had left the premises. Real Maddie
had finally said something she meant.

For a moment, Maddie watched the significance of the
comment dawn in Ashby's unnaturally blue eyes. In another blink, those eyes lit with angry fire. Ashby charged

at Maddie, shoving her backwards and tumbling into Nick, who had been leaning over examining the pies.

Maddie tried in vain to keep her balance, but the shove was vicious. She bounced off Nick's back and tumbled to the ground. Within seconds, two of the older judges, Mr. Floyd Prescott and Mr. Hollis Jones, had reached down in their immaculate summer suits to help her up.

Maddie immediately wished she'd stayed down. She stared in horror at the pie table. Each of Nick's hands had landed in a pie. His gray shirt was splattered with crust and whipped cream and berries. Even worse, his face was completely covered. The pie ladies and the other judges rushed to help, trying to right the remaining pies while keeping Nick from dripping berry juice all over the table.

At one time Maddie might have done something as impulsive as push Ashby back. But now she took a step away. When she looked at Ashby, she was holding a pie. Actually, she was a second away from launching it.

"Just put down the pie and walk away, and we'll let bygones be bygones." Maddie felt like she should be wearing a police uniform and holding a stun gun instead of contemplating arming herself with pies.

Ashby tossed her a defiant look and cranked up the pie.

"Let's just talk like civilized—"

Too late. Ashby tossed the pie, a direct hit to Maddie's face. The pie splattered all over—her hair, her clothes, blinding her and covering her nose so she couldn't breathe.

This was war.

Maddie scooped enough pie off her face so she could see. "Okay, I guess we're past talking."

Something devilish came over her, that feeling of pure

kicking-someone's-butt that she hadn't felt since she was nine and Derrick ambushed her Barbies with his GI Joes and held them for ransom money. Maddie picked up a certain pie from the table. One of Ashby's. It hovered in Maddie's hands like a Frisbee. Clearing both her pie eyes for good aim, she let it rip.

Fluffs of whipped cream spread everywhere, in Ashby's perfect hair and all over her designer sundress. Ashby froze, open-mouthed, in a state of shock. "How dare you? You little *whore*."

Nick placed himself in front of Maddie, sheltering her from any further airborne pies. "What exactly is going on here?"

Maddie lost all pretense of dignity as the words burst out. "She said you slept with her right after we broke up. Is that true?"

Nick glanced from one woman to another. "Ashby, give it up. I didn't sleep with you then, and I sure as hell am not going to now."

Ashby's jaw dropped open. *Better shut it so you don't let the flies in*, Grandmeel would say. The three of them stared at one another. Ashby's girlfriends who were helping man the pie booth flocked to her side.

"Nick," Maddie said. At the sound of her voice, he turned slowly, no doubt not wanting to leave his flank unguarded from new attacks.

"What is it?"

"Say that again." Tears clouded her eyes. She blinked hard and swallowed past the lump in her throat.

"Say what again?" He fully faced her now.

"The part about not sleeping with her."

"Maddie, I never slept with her."

"But after prom, you broke up with me. You dated *her*."

"We went out a couple of times. That was it."

All the hurt and betrayal she'd felt at eighteen came rushing back. "You crushed me."

No matter what he said, Maddie realized that she'd just stood up for her brokenhearted eighteen-year-old-self in a way she'd never had the courage to before. And that made her feel positively giddy.

The pie ladies were scrambling to the messed-up table, running and exclaiming and gesturing with their arms. Nick pulled Maddie out of the commotion, raked his fingers through the mess in his hair. "I knew I had to leave this town if I was ever going to make something of myself. I thought that if I dated Ashby, you wouldn't try to get back together. I wanted a fast simple break. So I cut the ties, quick and clean. Only it wasn't simple. Because here we are ten years later, and I still can't get you off my mind."

Maddie stared at him, tried to take in the truth of what he'd said. "You felt I would drag you down, stop you from accomplishing your goals? I was too small town for you?"

"No. It wasn't like that. I figured I didn't deserve you, a squeaky clean girl from the rich part of town, with your family telling you I was trailer trash."

"I never thought of you like that."

"I'm sorry, Maddie." He looked deep into her eyes and straight through to her soul. "I'm sorry I hurt you."

Shock and surprise mingled like all the tangy flavors of that pie.

He scooped a chunk of pie off her forehead and then licked his finger. A slow, wide smile spread on his face that weakened her knees and made her forget all about spiteful people and their pies.

"Madison Marie Kingston, your mama's pie is disqualified." Ashby's pronouncement echoed from the microphone and jarred Maddie out of her trance.

Insulting her was one thing, but her mother…Maddie stalked forward a few steps until she felt an arm catch at her elbow.

She resisted Nick's restraint. "This is the twentieth year my mom's entered this contest. I can't let it be my fault she's disqualified."

"Maddie," Nick said gently, "if you two get into it again, there's not going to be any pie tent, let alone contest."

She allowed him to steer her away, if only because his revelations buzzed relentlessly in her ears. *I didn't sleep with her. I didn't deserve you. I'm sorry.*

They stood in the back alley between the tents and the vendors where traffic was limited only to the fair workers. Nick held her tightly by both arms. "Maddie, listen to me. Look at me."

It was so hard with pie in her eyes and dripping off her hair. Nick's touch was firm but soothing at the same time. In any other circumstance, the contrast between all the deep red and white distraction covering his face and his determined expression would have made her burst out laughing.

"Let it go. Charging back in there will only make you look bad." His voice was calm, soft, and oh, so comforting, she wanted to wrap herself in it and hold tight.

Maddie shook her head vigorously. "I already look bad. No one in this town thinks I can run the company. Everyone thinks I'm a total screw-up."

"I don't." He shook her hard. "Look, when you're in the public eye, you get scandalized. People try to slam you. You have to be above it all. You have to have faith in yourself. That's what will get conveyed to other people. Not the slanderous words of someone out to get you."

Maddie smacked her head, only to have berry filling drop from her hair. "I ruined my mom's chances at the blue ribbon."

He laughed. The sound was as warm as his touch. "Yes, you did. But she'd be the first to tell you it was worth it to see the look on Ashby's face when you smashed that pie into it."

Suddenly Maddie laughed, too, not so much at Ashby but at the ridiculousness of the whole situation. So hard she snorted and doubled over, holding her stomach.

With one swift tug, Nick pulled her against him and covered her pie-smeared mouth with his. Lips met past layers of strawberry pie filling. Maddie's arms wrapped around his neck, his hands gripped her waist and stroked the soft, sensitive skin there. The hot, sweet taste of him mixed with the tart sweetness of the berries and all she could think was that she wanted more of him, all of him, right here and right now.

He drew back and licked a speck of whipped cream off his lip.

"What was that for?" she gasped, struggling to recover from the kiss.

"Just letting you know your pie face is a lot cuter than Ashby's."

"Really?"

"Yep." A goofy grin shone beneath the pie. "Hands down."

"Madison, what on earth has happened here? Ashby

threw a pie?" Mrs. Gorsky was standing next to them in back of the tent. She'd surely seen them kissing. Even the feathers on top of her hat appeared to chide.

Under the encrusted pie, Maddie felt her cheeks go warm. She glanced into the tent. Ashby was waving her arms, clearly upset. "Oh, Mrs. Gorsky. I'm so sorry. She did, but then I threw one of hers right back at her."

"Did you say it was one of *her* pies you used?"

"Yes, ma'am. It was unkind. I—"

"She shouldn't be entering the competition anyway since I put her in charge. But that is about to change right now. I think you should leave before this situation gets even more out of hand." Mrs. Gorsky's words sounded firm, but she patted Maddie gently on the arm.

Maddie breathed out in relief. "Yes, ma'am."

Mrs. Gorsky stalked back to the pie commotion. Nick tugged gently at Maddie's elbow.

She was grateful for not having to go back to the pie mess, and she definitely did not want to confront Ashby any further. But she had a dreadful feeling that following Nick would be even more dangerous.

Chapter Twelve

In a town where everybody knows everybody, even if you're covered with pie, it was all Nick could do to grab Maddie's hand and run for the hills—or at least cut through some yards to keep them off Main Street and away from all the gawking eyes as they ran back to her house.

They ran till they were laughing and out of breath and Maddie was holding her side with a cramp. Nick had the strange feeling that for once his heart was weightless. His cares seemed as remote as the din of the festival.

Maddie opened the kitchen screen door but Nick pulled her back. "Wait."

She looked at him with a puzzled expression. "We don't have much time to clean up before everyone comes back and starts getting ready for Grandmeel's party."

"Maybe we should rinse off first in the lake." He glanced down at his shirt, encrusted with stains and remnants of pie. "So we don't track this stuff through the house."

Maddie searched his face, her eyes asking a million questions. Maybe she was wondering if he remembered the last time they swam in that lake together. *Yes, he did. They were seventeen, and they skinny dipped.* Or if she was considering that kiss they'd just shared, that sticky, sugary, whipped-topping covered kiss that had burned its way right through his heart. *It was one hell of a kiss.* Maybe she was wondering if his intentions were honest, just to take a quick dunk and get all this pie off of them. *Well, they were not*, and she had every right to worry.

They walked down to the dock and kicked off their flip-flops, bare feet slapping along the wooden slats. Maddie ran almost to the end but stopped short of jumping in. She stood looking off into the distance where the tents and booths set up at the park stood in full view. The faint din of fiddle music drifted across the lake.

"What is it?" Nick asked.

She faced him, her expression serious. "I owe you an apology."

"For what?"

"Maybe I was wrong, pegging you as a cutthroat businessman. And I appreciate your support."

"I have a secret to tell you."

"What's that?"

"Don't tell anyone, but I'm not really all that cutthroat."

"You're not?"

He flashed a grin. "No. The part of my job I really enjoy is helping nonprofits get off the ground and thrive."

"Nonprofits?"

"I've done a lot of work with Children's Hospital."

"So that's why they chose you to be one of their

bachelors."

"That and the fact that I'm cute."

"Don't do that." She shook her head as if to shake off the spell he was casting over her. Blood coursed through his veins hard and fast at the hope that he *was* affecting her, maybe as much as she was affecting him.

"Don't do what?" he asked innocently.

"Don't make me like you again."

"Oh, admit it. You like me. *A lot.*"

"I totally didn't say that."

He waggled a finger in front of her face and she leaned away. "It's all over your face."

"What's all over my face? Pie?"

"Say it. Say you like me."

She crossed her arms. "I won't."

"Stubborn woman." He scooped her up and tossed her into the water, then dove in himself.

Nick heard whooping and hollering and splashing, and half of it was coming from him. When was the last time he'd laughed like this? She'd made him laugh more in the past two days than he had all year.

Nick swam up to Maddie and locked his arms around her. She uttered a surprised squeak. A dragonfly buzzed by, skimming the surface of the lake. The world went silent as they stood there, neck deep in the cool water, the hot sun warming their faces.

Maddie's laughter died. Her eyes were lighter blue than the water, closer in color to the summer sky than the lake, and they held flickers of challenge, of excitement, of worry. She always was a terrible liar, and now he realized why. Her eyes were so pure, so expressive. She wore all her feelings there.

"I have something else to say," he said. He ran a wet hand along her cheek, cradled her face in his hands.

"What is it?" Her lashes were flecked with tiny water drops. He had an impulse to kiss each one of them away.

Nick dropped his hands and stared at her. He sucked at words. He closed his eyes and tried to find the right ones, but when he opened them, he was still standing neck high in the lake and in trouble, and Maddie was waiting with those clear, guileless eyes.

"You're everything bright and light and kind. Everyone likes you. You belong to this town, and people will have confidence in you."

"So serious." She playfully smoothed away the frown lines between his eyes. Her touch made him shudder. He was in deep trouble. "But thanks for the support."

"I still don't have answers for our problems. But God help me, I can't stay away."

Her eyes went wide. He didn't know if he'd said the right thing. Hell, he just knew he didn't want to ruin the moment.

He wrapped one hand gently around the back of her neck, drawing her closer. "Maddie," he said low and soft, stroking one final fleck of pie off her cheek. "Maddie, I—"

He never got to finish the sentence. She grabbed him by the shoulders and leapt up, wrapping her legs around him and plastering her wet body against his. Her sweet lips locked with his and didn't let go.

They fit together just right, perfectly in tune as their kisses grew wetter and deeper. He plunged his tongue into her mouth, met hers, dove and possessed, and she was right with him all the way. Her hands pushed through his wet hair, clutched at his back, skimmed his shoulders. She pressed against him more and more urgently, and pushed her soft breasts up against his chest.

His hands dove under her floating shirt and skimmed those breasts, tracing each precious sphere and lingering over her taut nipples until she trembled beneath his touch.

He wanted to tell her this never felt so right, that having her back in his arms was like having that big crack in his heart sealed. For the first time in so long, he felt like a whole man again. But how could he? He had decisions to make, and either way, people would lose. He had the power to make or break both their families.

She must have sensed his hesitation. "Nick." Her voice was breathless, turned on. She reached up to caress his face as carefully as a rare piece of porcelain and looked lovingly and hungrily into his eyes. "Don't think, okay?" Her small hands worked magic, smoothing over the stubble on his chin, his neck. "Just for a little while."

When was the last time he didn't think? Was spontaneous?

A year ago. That one night. And his world had been upside down ever since.

His breath came in ragged heaves. The world dimmed, the lake and the sun and the fine summer day all distilled down to the fine taste of her, the feel of her soft, moist lips and the way her hands grazed his body underwater. When she grasped his cock, slowly traced its outline through his shorts, everything outside of them ceased to exist.

"Madison." He pushed a wet strand of hair off her face. "I want you. More than I've wanted anyone."

Suddenly the past was past, and he didn't want to waste a single second more.

"Nick." It was the softest whisper said on a mere exhale, but hearing her say his name so tenderly drove him to distraction. Her hands rode up his back and settled tightly around his neck. He wanted to take her now, right in the water, without another thought.

He reached between them to touch her flimsy little strip of lacy underwear. His fingers roamed underwater, slid between her silken curls. He wanted nothing but to bury himself deep inside her, right in the middle of this swampy lake with the high noon sun scorching down on them.

He slipped his finger into her silken wetness. She jerked a little in surprise but clung to him tighter, her inner muscles clasping as a second finger joined the first. Through his shorts, he felt her hand tug on his rigid cock. "Nick, let me—"

"Later. Just hold on," he said, his thumb stroking the center of her heat. The look she gave him, trusting, honest, willing, struck him in the heart. Stroke after stroke, he knew what she needed to go over the edge, and gave it until she clutched at him, pushed her body against his hand, and arched her back as she let go with a cry and shook with pleasure in his arms.

He covered her cry with kisses until her breathing finally slowed. She'd just slipped her hands under the waistband of his shorts when a sound cut through his haze of pleasure. Someone was calling Maddie's name.

He planted one last kiss on her forehead. "We'd better get back or we'll be late for that party."

She took a few wobbly steps. "What party?" she asked with a shaky laugh.

He lifted her into his arms and carried her to shore. On the dock, they made an attempt at squeezing out their sopping clothes.

"At least we got all the pie off," Maddie said.

They walked barefoot up the sloping lawn to the house, but as they got to the deck, Amelia stood, looking like an American flag in her red pants and crisp white blouse scattered with blue stars, tapping her red pumps impatiently on the deck.

"There you are. It's about time. The whole town is gossiping."

Nick hoped the gossip was about what happened before the lake, not in it. Not that they would have looked like much more than a few bright dots from the house, but he wouldn't put anything past Amelia.

Madison smoothed her wet hair from her face. Nick kept an arm lightly on her elbow. He wanted her to know he had her back, and he wasn't going to allow a disgruntled old lady to dictate to him. He hoped Maddie would stand up to her too.

Besides, they weren't teenagers sneaking around. They were nearly thirty-year-old adults. Grandmeel would have to get over it.

"I heard about the pie fiasco. I think you should know that despite your rather immature behavior, Ophelia Gorsky divested Ashby from the pie chairmanship and disqualified her pies from the competition. And she gave your mother the first-place ribbon."

"Oh, that's wonderful. I'm so glad."

"You owe her a thank-you. She could have banned your mother from ever entering again after the ruckus you caused."

"I didn't start it, Grandmeel." Maddie stopped, as if

finally realizing she didn't have to explain herself to her grandmother.

"It doesn't matter who started it. The fact remains you created a stir. How on earth are you going to function as the head of our town's largest business if you can't gain the respect of the people?"

"Grandmeel, I'm doing everything in my power to prove my loyalty to Kingston Shoes."

"I should remind you your loyalties are not to be found wrapped in the arms of a Holter, that's for damn sure." Amelia spun about and stalked to the house, her heels *clickety-clacking* along the deck.

Madison's face went white. She stood there, wet, clutching her stomach as if she'd just been punched.

Nick tried to hold in his outrage. "Don't let her do this to you. You were provoked in the worst way. Sometimes you have to fight back."

She crossed her arms, took a step away from him. "She's right. If I head up the company, my behavior has to be above reproach. The townspeople are expecting something big from me. I've promised to save their jobs, their livelihood. Not get in cat fights with someone who lives to aggravate me."

"You're too hard on yourself."

She creased her lips into a tight, unbelieving line. "Thank you for this afternoon." She pecked him on the cheek before she headed to the house.

When she got to the screen door, she turned. "I think it's best if we stay away from each other. Our business interests are still at odds, and this is another layer of complication neither one of us needs."

"Maddie, no."

"I've got responsibilities, Nick. I'm sorry."

As the door closed behind her, Nick's brain knew she was right, but his heart knew it was all wrong.

He paced, carefully avoiding tiny toy cars and action figures, back and forth along the redwood-stained deck. Suddenly, he halted. The same shot of adrenaline that always pumped through his veins at the onset of a brilliant idea flooded through him. He could help Maddie, all right—by doing what he did best.

He reached for his phone and realized he didn't have it. One quick curse later, he ran into the kitchen, which was thankfully vacant. He found the house phone, and punched in his partner and best friend's number.

"This had better be urgent." The irritated tones of a familiar Carolina accent rolled through the line.

"Hello, Preston, I'm fine, thanks. How are you?"

"It's Saturday night, and unlike you, I'm planning to enjoy every moment of these last two months before I ship out to Afghanistan." A distinctly female giggle permeated the background.

"I'm back home in Buckleberry."

Dead silence. The sound of footsteps. "Did someone die?"

"No, of course not. I'm here with Madison and her family for her grandmother's birthday."

"I've only had two beers, but I think I'm hearing things."

"It's a long story."

"Is Cat there? With the actuary?"

It had taken him all of sixty seconds for him to mention Cat. "His name is Robert, and he's her fiancé."

"We had drinks when he was crunching some numbers for that company we worked with in Chicago. All he talked about were his plans to trade pork bellies futures and how fast he can do the New York Times Sudoku every morning. I've never met someone so exacting and logical. It was like having a fucking conversation with Mr. Spock."

"Maybe she needs someone safe and predictable." Unlike Preston, a West Point grad with a penchant for women and danger. Preston was every mother's worst nightmare.

"Maybe." The line silenced except for a faint background of crackles. Nick had a feeling Preston wouldn't pursue the topic further. "Why'd you call, anyway?"

"I need to infuse some capital into one of our holdings."

He laid out the plan. Nick would give Maddie what she wanted most — success in running her company. Stability for her family. What that meant for his grandfather, he wasn't sure.

Or what it meant for *them*. Maddie had told him their getting together was a bad idea, but what if things were different? What if they weren't at odds, and what if the barriers between them could be removed?

Even as Nick hoped, he knew that Maddie needed a long-term kind of guy.

He wasn't that kind of guy, not even with her. *Especially* not with her. He wanted her badly, but he could not fall for her. He'd always sealed himself off from that danger, because someone was bound to get hurt — it was inevitable. And if he weren't careful, in this case it might be him.

Chapter Thirteen

Adjusting her skirt and smoothing down her just-straightened hair that was already going bonkers in the humidity, Maddie knocked hard on the front door of Samuel Holter's house. No answer.

She rubbed her fingers over her kiss-swollen lips. Just thinking of the afternoon with Nick made her tremble a little. Those hot, incredible kisses she had no business wanting or taking. But oh, she did want them. And so she needed answers, answers that would free both of them from the prison of the past. Maybe Samuel Holter could provide them.

Nick believed in her, even if her family didn't. He'd said it again at the lake. Now it was time for her to believe in herself, and her first task was going to be getting to the bottom of this feud, once and for all.

The tiny post-war house hadn't changed a bit from the one time she'd seen it as a kid. Back then she'd been shocked by its size compared to the rambling colonial where she'd grown up. It seemed to underscore the long-reaching aftershocks of the rift between their families. But she'd never held that against Nick. If anything, he had felt a super-sensitiveness about it that had driven a wedge between them no matter how much she'd told him it didn't matter.

There was an old blue Chevy Malibu in the driveway, and the small side door to the garage was open, so she headed there. She passed bright red geraniums growing in blue ceramic pots and a big American flag that hung vertically from the porch. Hadn't Nick's granddad been a Vietnam vet?

No one occupied the small, pristine garage. To her amazement, in addition to the usual rakes and brooms and tools tidily lined up on hooks, it held a magnificent workspace with an architect's desk and a long table covered with drawings.

Drawings of *shoes*.

Maddie collapsed into a swivel chair, stunned. On the slanted surface of the desk, and filling a long table beside it, were sketches, one after another, of high heels, flats, sexy, satiny pumps with bead and pearl embellishments, casual lace-up shoes and boots. Done in charcoal, pastel, watercolor. Design after design, each one unique and beautiful.

An artist? Maddie scanned her memories. She knew Sam Holter used to manage three Happy Shoe stores, Kingston Shoes' major regional competitor. But a shoe designer?

A strange frizzle of a thrill pulsed through her, a discovery that seemed more a piece of an old puzzle than a new one, one that should have been put together long ago. She felt deep in her bones she was looking at something big and significant.

Did Nick want his grandfather to be in charge of the

business? It would be the ultimate revenge. The Holters would get the last laugh. After all those years, their justice would finally be served.

Next to the drawings sat two shoes, half made, with a wedge heel and beautiful pale pink ribbons made to be tied at the ankle. Maddie touched the fine satin. Oh, they were beautiful, with the tiniest row of pearls running along the toe piece.

Maybe they would fit her. She smoothed her hand along one beautifully shaped arch, appreciated the pale blush color, how the ribbons were threaded carefully through tiny jute loops. She slipped off one of her own shoes and slowly slid her foot into the gorgeous one.

"May I help you, young lady?" a gruff voice said.

Maddie dropped the shoe. Shame colored her face as she scrambled to stand. She felt like Goldilocks caught with porridge on her face. And here was the great big bear.

She'd seen Sam Holter enough times in the past to know who he was, but even if she hadn't, his resemblance to Nick was uncanny. He had Nick's build, his carriage. Tall and strong, he was a good-looking man with silver hair and tanned skin. And an expression as formidable as Grand-meel's. He was holding a garden trowel in one hand and a wilted geranium in the other.

"The shoes," she whispered. "They're beautiful."

Thick brows deepened in a V between steely blue eyes. "You're the Kingston girl."

Well, she wasn't a *girl* anymore, but she was anxious to get on his good side, if he had one. So she let the slightly condescending comment slide.

"Yes, Mr. Holter, I'm Maddie." She held out her hand,

but he didn't move to take it. To be fair, he did have his hands full. "The door was open and I—I got distracted by all the drawings."

"If you're looking for Nick, he's not here." He set the geranium pot down and gave her the eyeball.

Well, she could scrutinize right back. Who on earth planted geraniums when it was ninety-five degrees?

"I came to chat with you."

"Chat?" He said it like she wanted to give him vaccinations. Multiple ones.

Maddie scanned the garage. A standing fan provided some air circulation, but it still felt like a greenhouse in full sun. An old radio and a coffee mug sat in the corner of the table, within reach of the desk. This was clearly his sanctuary.

She ignored the sweat rolling between her shoulder blades. "You're a neat freak like your grandson."

He shrugged, pulled up an old metal stool, and perched on it. "Order staves off the disorder of the rest of life."

She thought of Nick, so tightly in control. To the world, he projected a cocky self-confidence, a calm, laid-back demeanor. She wondered if he ever let anyone close enough to see what was underneath.

"It couldn't have been easy, what happened to your family."

He shook his head. "Nicky, he was a good boy. We took care of each other. He deserved a lot more than a clueless old man to raise him."

"He thinks very highly of you, Mr. Holter. He'd do anything for you."

She didn't want Nick to be the enemy. Or his grandfather, for that matter. She wanted all of this to be over. She wanted a *chance*.

Dear God, she wanted a chance with Nick. A real, honest-to-goodness fresh-start chance, where they could be together and give in to all the tumultuous feelings that kept her so off balance.

"I'm proud of everything Nicky's done. I just— "

Maddie looked up.

"Are you in love with my grandson, Miss Kingston?"

Her breath caught. Blood pounded through her body, propelled by a heart that reacted too wildly even at the mention of the charismatic, sexy hunk that was Nick Holter. She could never betray her family for a man, not even if that man was Nick. What kind of daughter would she be? "I—I don't know."

"That's the problem with young people these days. No passion. No commitment."

"I have both—for my family. Nick's buying my father's company for *you*, isn't he?"

"That's nonsense." He sounded irritated, but something more…surprised.

"He owns nearly half our shares. That's why I brought him back this weekend, so he could see the consequences if he dismantles the company and takes everyone's jobs. But now I think maybe he just wants to put you in charge."

"I retired from the shoe business many years ago, young lady." Sam Holter wagged an arthritic finger. "I have no desire at my age to be in charge of a company."

"But what about all this?" She waved her arms over his workspace.

He snorted and held up the beautiful shoe she'd just admired. "Did you know I designed the orthopedic sole used in all of your company's shoes?"

She shook her head.

"Well, your grandfather's idea was always to sell comfortable, sensible shoes. But I was more...artistic. I always wanted to figure out how to make a beautiful shoe that felt great, too."

Maddie raised a brow at the sky-high wedge. "This is comfortable?"

"Try it on."

He didn't have to ask her twice. She slipped on the satin-covered shoe and tied the lovely pink ribbons. "Well, it's a little small, but it's light. The thickness of the sole prevents the foot from angling too much, and it's super cushioned under the ball of the foot."

"You sound like you know shoes."

Maddie shrugged. "I'm a Kingston."

He began rummaging in a cabinet behind his worktable. She glimpsed more pairs of shoes lined up in neat rows. Brilliant, beautiful shoes in a rainbow of colors. Her mouth watered.

"There are many times in life we don't get what we want." Samuel watched her with eagle eyes, as dark and discerning as Nick's. "What we do when we're confronted with things we didn't get, what we lost—those are the times that show what we're made of."

"I—I'm not sure what you're telling me." Her voice was a coarse, clogged whisper. Was he talking about himself?

"Nick lost a lot as a boy. Sometimes I think it's a lot easier for him to be a big success than to take other risks. Personal ones."

"Are you telling me to fight for your grandson?"

"You have to decide that, Missy." The glance he leveled at her was loaded with age and wisdom and a little bit of suspicion, too. "Oh, you're not sure, that's what you said, right? The whole thing's just too complicated. Hell, if you play your cards right, we can drag this feud out another fifty years."

She rolled her eyes. "The feud wasn't our fault."

"I've moved on from it. Now you should too."

"Well, it's a little hard, considering your grandson is about to buy us out."

"Pish-posh," the old man said, waving his hand dismissively. "My Nicky's a good boy. He's not going to ruin you stubborn Kingston people because of an old feud."

Clearly, Gramps hadn't heard the Nick-Holter-is-a-Cold-Blooded-Shark stories.

"He wants you to have your dream," Maddie said.

"I'm too old for that now."

"Mr. Holter, what if I told you I'm a graphic designer, and I'm in love with shoes and all I do in my spare time is draw them?"

He crossed his big arms defensively but one of his craggy eyebrows lifted a little as Maddie continued.

"In my job, I draw shoes for ads, but I'm always embellishing, improving, creating my own designs. Trouble is, I haven't got a clue about insoles and engineering and comfort, all the stuff you're an expert at. If we could create a shoe that's beautiful yet feels good, maybe we could have a shot at *this*." Maddie pulled a folded paper out of her purse. "It's a design competition. If I win, I could get the company out of the red."

"Why should I help your company, young lady?"

"Look, I don't know why that feud started, but my

grandfather's gone and my family and the whole town need Kingston Shoes to continue. And maybe you want another shot at showing the world what you've got. If we work together, maybe we can win."

Samuel paused a long time. Finally he sighed. "You got drawings?"

Maddie drew her hands together in an excited little clap. "Oh, boy, have I got drawings."

"Then I'll look at them, but only because you're a pretty girl and you've got lots of chutzpah coming to see me like this."

Maddie ran over and hugged him. "Oh, thank you! This is wonderful!" She glanced at her phone. Five p.m. "Oh, I've got to go. It's my grandmother's birthday party tonight at The Lodge, and I can't be late."

The old man's face crumpled. "Amelia's turning seventy-two, is she?" Another long pause. "Well, you must wish her a happy birthday for me."

"Of course." Maddie stooped to kiss him on the cheek. "And I *will* be back to try on more shoes."

"I bet you're an eight and a half."

"How'd you know that?"

He shrugged. "Kingstons might know shoes, but Holters know women. At least their feet."

Shocking. Sam Holter wasn't bitter or angry. In fact, once you got past the general crotchetiness, he was really quite…pleasant.

He didn't seem out to rule a shoe empire, even if his grandson presented it to him on a silver platter. Maybe Holters knew women, but Maddie had to wonder just how well Nick knew his own grandfather.

Chapter Fourteen

Nick needed a drink before he faced the evening, the next test of this long weekend from hell. As he sat at the long banquet table at The Lodge, Derrick couldn't stop talking about his new recruits. Cat barely spoke to Robert and looked like she was about to cry. Amelia roosted at the head, wearing diamonds, drinking wine, and preparing to be feted.

Around them, the restaurant bustled amid the low hum of conversation and clinking silverware. Rustic woodwork and flickering candlelight accented the fabulous view of Lake Watchacatchee. The familiar smell of cedar permeated the air, well remembered from Nick's busboy days.

Nick glanced at his watch. He hadn't seen Maddie since their dip in the lake. She'd been gone for hours and having his cell phone under government arrest wasn't helping.

His mind replayed the afternoon. Maddie's sweet body wrapped around him tightly, her wet, soft lips sliding over his, their skin cool and slippery as things heated up in the water. If Granny hadn't shown up, he had no doubt they'd have escaped to Maddie's bedroom and finished what they'd started.

Maddie had wrapped herself around his brain and short-circuited it in a way no other woman had ever done before. Nick unbuttoned his top button under his tie and cleared his throat. It was no use. He couldn't clear his mind of her. He didn't want to think about shoes or grandparents or feuds. He was done with berry festivals and birthday dinners and smiling for brothers who eyed him like he was about to steal the family silver.

He wanted her, plain and simple.

But first he had to survive this abominable party.

He rose from his seat and meandered over to the bar. Damned if Derrick didn't take the seat next to him.

"Thought we could have a man-to-man," Derrick said as he ordered them each a beer. Nick wished for something a lot stronger.

"Okay," Nick said warily. "What about?"

"My grandmother said she saw you two making out in the lake."

Nick choked on his swig. Orneriness overcame him, making him feistier than usual. Or maybe sex-deprivation was just making him short tempered. "Maddie's not a child." It was the first edgy thing he'd said all weekend, and he didn't regret it.

"No, but she's my sister. I don't want to see her hurt."

"That's laudable."

"Just because I'm tough on her doesn't mean I don't love her."

"No, of course not," Nick said. "Just that I think you

should give Maddie more credit. She's got a lot on her plate, and she's managing pretty damn well."

Derrick laughed. "My sister can't be the boss of anyone. She's too soft. Hell, when she was a counselor at Camp Watchacatchee, she let her cabin of teenagers have a party on the last night, and they ended up painting the cabin walls with shaving cream and painting her toenails with toothpaste. When she taught Sunday school, she brought finger paints for the preschoolers, and they painted each other's Sunday clothes. When she dressed the mannequins at Macy's, she and a coworker paired them up and decked them in rainbows for a gay pride parade that passed by and she lost her job. Her heart's in the right place, but she has no leadership skills."

"You mean she doesn't have *black and white* leadership skills."

Nick contemplated that. Hadn't Maddie accused him of either/or thinking? She was rubbing off on him, and he wasn't sure if that was a good thing. So this time he took a double swig.

Derrick frowned. "I'm an Army captain, Nick. If my company doesn't obey, lives are at stake. I can't abide disobedience. Sometimes conformity means order."

"Maybe you should tolerate nonconformity in this case. Maddie cared about your family's company enough to quit a job she loved to come and save it. That's pretty damn out-of-the-box if you ask me."

It was instinct for Nick to rise to Maddie's defense, but this time it wasn't blind teenage love that made him want to play Lancelot to her Guinevere.

Maddie was the best person to take over this sad, ailing company. She had the passion, dedication, and loyalty to her family and the people of her town to do it. Because that's what Maddie did. She gave everything her all. When you had Maddie's love in your corner, you had her loyalty. All one hundred fifty percent of it. He couldn't even wrap his head around what it would be like being in the circle of all that love. Belonging was something he'd never experienced.

Derrick seemed agitated. "Maddie was able to up and quit her job. She doesn't have a family to support."

For the first time, Nick sensed a reason for Derrick's barbs. Could it be he felt as helpless as Maddie during their family's crisis? "You're doing what you can, just like your sisters. It's a tough situation."

"Yeah, you've got that right." Derrick finally took a swig of his beer. Not a big admission, but Nick felt Derrick's bristles retract just a little.

Jenna ran over, cell phone in hand, talking animatedly about a problem with the babysitter, and pulled Derrick away. Robert scraped back Derrick's empty bar stool and sat down heavily. Judging by the way he scrubbed his hand over his face and slumped into the seat, something was wrong.

"Bartender, two whiskeys. Straight up," Nick said. Finally, he'd get a real drink. Nick slapped Robert on the back. "What's up, friend?"

"Cat just told me she gave five thousand dollars of our wedding money to Maddie for some charity event. For her sister's pet project or something. I mean, who does that?"

Nick raised a brow. "She must be pretty passionate about the charity."

The heavy shot glasses clicked on the smooth surface of the bar as the bartender set them down. Nick nodded thanks and handed one to Robert.

"She said it was some stupid bachelor auction Cat took part in for the children's hospital. I kept asking her why so much? She said I didn't understand and it was important to Maddie. But what about me, dude? Aren't I important?"

Whoa. Nick downed his own drink and relished the slow burn and flare.

Maddie must have been desperate to win him. Had she believed that strongly she could change his mind? Or was she simply down to her last scheme?

He would never conduct his own affairs that way. Business was cut and dry. It was all about profit margins and cutting losses. It wasn't about emotions, family ties, and sentimentality.

Was it?

"And Granny Vader over there…" Robert nodded toward Amelia, who was standing by a tableful of presents greeting family. "Is the saddest excuse for a grandmother I've ever met. She called me Alex P. Keaton and told Cat she'd better take some risks in life or she'll die of boredom. Imagine that!"

Nick looked up, and suddenly there stood Madison, in the doorway next to her mother, pushing her father's wheelchair. She wore a black and white skirt that hugged her hips and a black blouse and sexy black heels, her hair up and not a trace of pie anywhere. She scanned the room, searching…and locked gazes with him. His heart filled with that achy-breaky feeling like it was overloaded with something too heavy to handle. That should have been a warning to look away, but instead he found himself smiling and flashing a little wink that made her cheeks go pink.

It pleased him to see her a little rattled. Nick walked up to them, kissed Maddie lightly on the cheek, and shook her father's hand. "Mr. Kingston. Good to see you again."

Henry Kingston was pale and could use another twenty or so pounds on his big frame, but his grip was surprisingly firm.

"Nicholas, Maddie has told me you're touring the company tomorrow and are going to offer us some suggestions."

"I'll do what I can, sir." It was the truth. He wasn't some ogre that wanted to wreak havoc in people's lives. High management came with high stress and hard decisions. Nick understood that only too well, even as he squelched the sudden urge to snatch Maddie up and haul her out over his shoulder far away from all their problems.

Maddie pecked her grandmother on the cheek. "Happy birthday, Grandmeel."

Amelia eyed her granddaughter with her usual skepticism. "Well, I must say your outfit tonight is a bit revealing, Madison."

Next to him, Maddie tensed. Her silky black blouse ran to a tasteful V, bearing just a hint of her gorgeous breasts—definitely not in any way skanky. Maybe Grandma was commenting on her black and white patterned skirt that clung to her beautiful derrière and black high heels that showed off her tanned, toned legs. He considered saying *my kind of outfit* but refrained.

Cat came to her rescue. "Gran, Maddie looks cute and tasteful. Leave her be."

"In my day we didn't wear skirts that clung to our backsides with such...enthusiasm." She turned to her other granddaughter. "Catherine, you look particularly lovely tonight. That pink dress with the pearls...classic. But where did that beau of yours get off to?"

Cat cleared her throat and looked down at her plate. "I think Robert had some business to tend to."

"Those boring insurance predictions he makes all day long? A woman needs to pick a man who offers her a sense of adventure."

Cat bit her bottom lip and took a sip of wine.

Maddie stepped in. "Grandmeel, perhaps adventure is in a person's heart, not just in the job they do. Did you have adventures with Gramps?"

"An adventure with him was discovering something exciting about a shoe trend. That business was his life. All I'm saying is you've got to pick a man who treasures you above all else. Treats you special. If you find that, you shouldn't ever let it get away. And Jenna, dear." Jenna looked up, startled, from her cell phone. Not even she would escape Amelia's harsh examination. "We'll attribute your lack of fashion sense to the fact that you are busy chasing after those rambunctious twins. And they are ever so very rambunctious, aren't they?"

Nick looked around the table. People were drinking, shifting in their seats uncomfortably, yet they all had smiles plastered onto their faces. What was it about this family that they were all so willing to allow this grandmother to tear into everyone?

"Oh, Grandmeel, please do not start on the next generation." To his surprise, it was Maddie. Jenna shot her a grateful look.

"I have expectations for my grandchildren is all. And great grandchildren. What's wrong with that?"

Fortunately, no one had to answer, because appetizers were served. As if they hadn't eaten enough berries earlier in the day, the dinner was berry themed, too—raspberry gazpacho, berry salad, halibut with a blackberry-ginger glaze. After having his entire body coated in berries, Nick wasn't too thrilled about eating them for every course, but Maddie was next to him and somehow he didn't really care if he was eating rocks for dinner. His shoulder grazed hers a few times on accident. He itched to grab her hand under the table, intertwine his fingers with hers, send her sweet, knowing glances about potential activities they could partake in with one another later after this treacherous meal was done.

But he wouldn't, and she was right. Things were complicated enough. He would have to be patient.

"Now that my Henry is here, we can truly celebrate," Grandmeel said, patting her son's hand. "Let's all have some berry wine."

"Thank you, Mother," Maddie's father said, picking up his wine glass. "I'd like to make a toast. To family. I want to take this opportunity, as you all came from so far away to celebrate your grandmother's birthday, to tell you how very proud I am of each and every one of you."

Maddie's eyes glistened. "Thank you, Daddy."

"Even if there is a Holter at the table," Amelia said.

Maddie's mom blanched, but she managed a smile as she tipped her glass toward Nick. "Yes, Amelia, even with Nicholas at our table, where he is very welcome."

Nick smiled and tipped his glass back before a voice interrupted the conversation.

"Actually, now there are two. Holters, I mean."

Everyone's head cranked up in unison to see an elegant silver-haired man in a jacket and tie who'd just announced himself.

Nick's grandfather had arrived just in time for dinner.

Chapter Fifteen

The sound of breaking glass caused Maddie's head to spiral back to Grandmeel. Deep red wine stained the fine white table linens. For the first time in her life, her grandmother was pale as her napkin, hands shaking as she tossed it to hide the spill and slowly stood.

For the first time, Amelia Kingston looked aged.

"Samuel. Samuel Holter." Her voice sounded shaky and panicked, like she was living her worst nightmare. "What in God's name are you doing at my birthday party?"

"I came to wish you happy birthday, Amelia. And to get a few things straight—for our grandchildren."

"My God, Samuel, can we not do this privately?"

"I've tried to, but you haven't returned any of my calls. I figured you might grant me an audience in public."

Samuel spoke eloquently and far more formally than he had in his garage, looking, in his suit, like the true Southern gentleman. But why would he show up here, with the entire family present?

Maddie grabbed Nick's hand, whispered *Do something!* into his ear. Her dad, her dad. What if Sam Holter spilled the beans about the business being in trouble?

Nick opened his mouth but Maddie's father spoke first. "Samuel, I have to ask that you continue this conversation another time. It's my mother's birthday."

"I apologize, Henry, but I feel my message is important enough that everyone should be privy to it."

Derrick's gaze flitted back and forth like he was watching a tennis match. Jenna focused on the table. Cat sat with her mouth open, staring at their father. Maddie's mom and dad took each others' hands, worried expressions on their faces.

Amelia balled her hands into fists, but she didn't look angry—she looked scared. "Why are you here?" Her voice actually shook.

"It's time for the feud to stop. It's gone on long enough, and it's affecting our grandchildren."

"I am not going to make up with you so my granddaughter can feel better about dating your grandson."

"We missed our chance at being together, Amelia. Let's not let that be the instrument that keeps our grandchildren apart."

Maddie choked on her wine. *Wait a minute.* They *missed* their *chance at being together?* "Grandmeel, you dated *him*?" The words burst out of her mouth before she could bite them back. Her grandmother's face went from paper white to scarlet red.

Amelia glanced about at each of her grandchildren, then at Samuel. "Do you see what you've started?"

"It's for the best," Samuel said softly.

"They are free to make their own choices, Samuel. Always have been."

"I'm talking about my Nicholas and your Maddie, Amelia. And I disagree."

Dear God. Everyone's gaze focused on the two of them. Maddie shifted uncomfortably in her seat. Fortunately Nick spoke, holding his hands up in a pacifying gesture. "We're fine, Gramps. No worries here."

"Yes, we're as friendly as they come, aren't we, Nick?" Maddie concurred with a nervous laugh.

They smiled big phony smiles at each other. Silently, Maddie prayed, *please, God, please don't let him tell my father the true state of the confederacy. It would kill him, just when he's nearly out of rehab.*

"They're making decisions about the company and about each other," Samuel said. "They should know the truth."

"Oh, all right. Fine." Grandmeel plunked herself down hard in her chair. Jenna handed her another glass of wine, and she took a big gulp before she spoke.

"We met at a party, he and I." She looked right at Samuel. "You were new in town. I didn't know anything about shoes or companies or partnerships. You were just a charming, handsome young man who asked me to dance."

"I fell in love with you at first sight."

Oh, this was so not good. Maddie's gaze shifted in panic from her grandmother to Nick's grandfather. She forced down a huge swallow of her own wine, bracing herself for whatever was next. Nick kept his eyes on their grandparents, but squeezed Maddie's hand under the table. The smallest gesture but it meant everything.

"Your parents weren't pleased," Samuel said. "I hadn't gone to college. The business was just getting started."

"But you worked hard. You created the designs, and Joe figured out how to sell them. You and Joe were a great team."

"Until Vietnam."

No one spoke. Maddie held her breath and gripped Nick's hand.

At last Amelia spoke. "Two years I waited." She gave a little shrug and stared at her plate. "I was lonely. Joe wore me down."

"I came back to find you married to my best friend."

Maddie's heart dropped like the sharp edge of a guillotine. She felt like they were all sitting on the inside of a bubble, where people outside talked and laughed, and waiters ran by with plates of food. But in their vacuum, all was cold, dead silence.

Grandmeel stood and looked around at the family. Her commanding posture was back, and all traces of any real emotion were erased from her eyes. "So there you have it. I was the reason for the feud."

She rose silently and left the table.

Maddie felt like she'd just been tazed. The tawdry truth was out. Once upon a time, a love triangle had broken up a company. There'd been fallout and casualties. For all Grandmeel's steely demeanor, Maddie had seen the moment when a look of sheer despair had filled her eyes. It had only lasted a second, but for the first time Maddie realized that maybe her grandmother, not Samuel Holter, might have been the hardest hit victim of them all.

• • •

"Grandmeel, are you all right?"

Out in back of the Lodge, it smelled like kitchen exhaust and grilled meat. Rusty hinges creaked as the old screen door slammed behind Maddie. Voices volleyed back and forth in the kitchen and pots and pans clanged. Grandmeel had somehow commandeered a cigarette and was smoking, something Maddie had not seen her do since she was seven and her granddad had died.

"Of course I am. Now get yourself back to dinner."

"Grandpa wasn't your true love, was he?"

"I declare, child, you are so tenacious. Just like the time you found that stray dog and badgered us all until you were allowed to keep it."

"You love Hughie."

"That is beside the point. I am *begging* you to go back to the dinner table."

"You've been angry all these years because you made a mistake. A mistake that cost you everything."

"Your grandfather was a good man." Her voice shook as she defended her husband. "He deserved to have a wife who loved him, and I did, until the day he died."

All those years of covering up, of pretending, that could make a person nasty. And cantankerous. Maddie put a hand on her grandmother's slender shoulder. "I'm so sorry, Grandmeel."

She blew out a pillar of cigarette smoke as elegantly as if she were Greta Garbo in a 1930s movie.

"It's best to stay away from Holter men. Do you

understand me? It's what I've been trying to tell you. Nick's on the other side, Madison. He'll ruin our company. He'll kill your poor father. And he'll break your heart."

Maddie stared at her grandmother—still so elegant and refined—and saw her in an entirely different light. She'd made a mistake that couldn't be undone, and it had cost her dearly.

She was still the opinionated, controlling, self-centered woman she'd always been, but she didn't have control over Maddie's life. Not anymore.

"No." The word echoed off the brick building in the spotlight where the two women stood. Moths flew crazily, unable to stop seeking the light. "The past is past, Grandmeel. We need to figure out how not to let it ruin our futures."

"My life is nearly done, but contrary to what you might believe, I want you to end up with someone good and kind, who treats you well, and can provide for you."

"I can provide for myself, Grandmeel. And I can decide this for myself, too." Maddie was tired of deception and lies and old, old quarrels that had forced her feelings about Nick at bay. "The past is dead. We need to start fresh."

"Where are you going?" her grandmother asked.

Maddie barely noticed that she'd started walking across the expanse of lawn between the Lodge and the lake.

"That boy will be the ruination of all of us." Her voice carried in the humid air.

Maddie turned about briefly to speak. "I'm sorry, Grandmeel. I have to live my life as I see fit, not as you see it for me."

"Madison Marie, don't you dare leave like this. You'll be sorry for your defiance!"

Maddie headed off down the hill, Grandmeel's voice nothing but a faint echo over the commotion of crickets.

Chapter Sixteen

Maddie traipsed through the dew-damp grass then wobbled on her heels down the long, tree-lined drive that wound back down to the street to town. There was no moon, and it looked like rain, but the endless blanket of woods surrounding her was comforting. A few cars passed, but she ducked between trees when they did, in no mood to be found by any Good Samaritans who might offer a ride.

She'd grown up thinking her grandparents had always hated the Holters, but in reality it had been the opposite. Her grandmother had loved Samuel Holter once, and maybe part of her still did. Yet she hadn't waited. Was it because she was young and lonely and heartsick and her grandfather had comforted her? Wooed her away? Or did it happen spontaneously, after months of resisting, when she finally gave in, then realized much, much later she'd made the worst mistake of her life?

Or was she as shallow and selfish as she was now, playing

with two men's emotions like a spoiled toddler with too many toys?

No one would know. And really, did it matter? All Maddie knew was that she was done listening to the advice of someone who'd allowed bitterness to eat up everything good about her. She was tired of being told who and why not to love.

She wanted to make her own decisions, her own mistakes. Not just about Nick, but about the company. It was time she stepped in and took charge and stopped trying to please everyone.

At the end of the winding drive, Maddie pulled her shoes off her tortured feet and tossed them far into the woods. Blisters burned on her heels and toes. Her stomach rumbled, not having eaten one bite of that very berry dinner. Just as well. She didn't care to see another berry for a long, long time.

Patsy Yates from the Five and Dime offered her a ride home, but she thanked her anyway and kept walking. Thunder rumbled in the distance and bright shots of heat lightning lit up the heavy skies. She hadn't gone more than half a block when she heard the soft putter of a car behind her.

Nick. Behind the wheel of the rented Accord.

"How did you find me?" she asked as he pulled up beside her.

Grinning, he shook his head. "When are you ever going to learn I have my ways, darlin'? This is my third pass through town. Must have missed you on that driveway somewhere."

Humor glinted from his deep brown eyes. God, he was so damn good-looking. He'd tossed off his jacket and tie. His skin was darkly tan against the whiteness of his shirt, the collar open at the throat, his arms muscular and strong against rolled-up cuffs as they firmly clutched the wheel.

Maddie held back the urge to leap into the car and smother him with kisses, tell him everything on her mind. Her crazy, unreliable heart wanted to give in, but it had gotten her into big, crazy trouble in the past and she didn't want to screw up again. So many uncertainties. But if she couldn't trust him, and she couldn't trust herself, who was left?

"Why don't you get in?" Nick's voice was low and cajoling. "A woman shouldn't be walking alone at night around here."

She laughed. "Right. The last crime in Buckleberry Bend was a year ago when someone's dog dug up the petunias around General Pritchett's statue."

"See? Wild dogs loose in town. You never know." He reached over and opened the door.

Just as Maddie grabbed hold of it, the clouds burst open and released torrents of rain. She jumped quickly into the car.

"Nick." She stared at his handsome face as the rain rattled and pinged off the roof. Her heart felt full as a water balloon in her chest, aching to burst and let everything out, all the emotion she'd been holding and hiding and denying. "Everything is so complicated. I—"

"No." He reached over and pulled her against him. Her cheek hit rock solid chest, inhaled spicy man-cologne and soap and the warm skin smell she'd always associate with him and only him. Once she'd stolen his sweater and tucked it under her pillow for a month before she gave it back for this very reason.

She wrapped her arms around the lean planes of muscle

on his back and clung on for all she was worth. The clatter-ing rain insulated them from the rest of the world, the world of Kingstons vs. Holters. Here, in this car, there was only the two of them, Maddie and Nick, and not one other thing mat-tered. Maddie lifted her face and he was right there, smooth-ing down her hair, tracing a finger slowly down her cheek and cradling her face tenderly in his big hands.

Warm waves of pleasure rolled through her, and she wrapped her arms more tightly around him. She never wanted to move again.

"Maddie." Nick said her name with finality, like it was a long-searched-for answer. His eyes drilled straight into her, a lethal mix of desire and tenderness that undid her totally. "I want you so bad I can't stand it."

At last. Relief coursed through her as her eyes grew misty and her throat caught. "I want you too." He crushed his mouth urgently over hers, their tongues searching and colliding until every part of her was breathless and shak-ing. He tasted like berry wine and comfort, planting kisses that were tangy and sweet and reminded her not of the sad, uncomfortable scene in the restaurant, but of sunshine and heat and the pure pleasure of being home after far too long away.

His lips broke from hers to trail down her neck, play in the hollow between her neck and shoulder. She had things she wanted to say, *had* to say, but her brain was short-circuit-ing under the sensual assault. Oh, those soft and skillful lips, those hands that wrapped tightly around her waist and crept up, up, ever so slowly just as she was going down under his hypnotic spell where nothing else mattered.

No. She wasn't young and impulsive anymore, all the

things that had gotten her so into trouble in the past, no matter how badly she wanted Nick. She pulled back, flattened her hands against his big chest.

Nick felt her hesitation. "Don't listen to your grandmother."

His hands reached the sides of her breasts, roamed over the lace of her bra. She shuddered. "We have to talk." Her voice came out sounding weak and dazed.

He swept her hair off her shoulder and nuzzled her neck. "Later," he murmured.

Maddie bit back a groan. "This is serious business."

"I am very serious." His hands roamed slowly over her breasts, making them grow heavy and sensitive.

"I need to tell you something." She gathered up his hands and held them hostage in hers.

He sighed and sat up. "All right, talk."

"I—had an idea for a compromise."

"A compromise. Working together. Closely. Let's start now." He dove back to nibbling on her neck.

"Nick!" She gave him a firm push. "You were right. Our company hasn't kept up with the times. The shoes are awful. No one our age would touch them. If you give me six months to try and turn the company around, I'll hire your grandfather to work with me on new designs. We'll create a new business plan, and you can have input. Everyone keeps their jobs, the company doesn't get dissolved, and we put our heads together to make it work. What do you say?"

Nick frowned. "You spoke to my grandfather?"

"He's very talented. I understand what you're trying to do, but he doesn't want to run a company. He wants to design shoes. Like me." Something loud snapped inside her head. Suddenly, things shone crystal clear and simple.

She pounded her palm emphatically against her chest. "*I* want to design shoes. Your grandfather's got what I need to jumpstart the business."

"Maddie Girl, it all sounds fine to me." He scootched up closer and started doing that neck thing again. Maddie bit her lip to try and stay rational, but it was getting hard.

"Just like that?"

Nick pulled back and looked at her so intently she was afraid the dream was about to end.

"What is it?"

He exhaled deeply. "Remember last year? The convention?"

She nodded. How could she not remember that night? It was tattooed on her brain and in her heart. For better or worse, there was no forgetting it.

"Running into you was no accident. I heard you were going to be there and I looked you up."

No accident? She swallowed hard. "W-Why?"

"I heard about your failed engagement. I wanted to see you." His expression was serious, his gaze honed in and focused. "I wanted to claim you for myself."

"What?" Her heart knocked hard against her chest, so loudly that maybe she hadn't heard him right.

"Then my grandpa had that health scare, and all that guilt came rushing back. I decided you and I were just too complicated. But you're in my blood, Maddie. I want a solution now. More importantly, I want you."

His words washed over her like the full-body relief of plunging into the lake on a hundred degree day. He wanted her now, and he'd wanted her a year ago. The revelation wrung her out and bowled her over at the same time.

Nothing can stop you now, a voice in her head said. *Go for it. Now. Don't waste a minute more on things past.*

Create a future.

"Take me home," she said, just before Nick covered her mouth with his and all her thoughts scattered.

The house was dark as they pulled up the drive. Maybe somehow everyone had managed to stay at The Lodge and have dinner after all. Maddie flicked on a few low lights. Nick hadn't said anything, and now he was propped against the kitchen counter, arms folded, a neutral look on his face. He'd put the ball in her court in every way.

She walked over to him and silently took up his big warm hand, then led him up the darkened staircase to her bedroom door.

Nick leaned over her, rested his hand above her on the doorjamb. His dark eyes smoldered with desire. "Can I come in?"

Maddie met Nick's fiery gaze. She turned the knob slowly behind her until the door clicked open. With one quick tug, she pulled Nick inside and shut the door behind them.

Chapter Seventeen

Nick took that as a *yes*. He captured Maddie's luscious mouth and plunged his tongue in like he wanted to plunge into her body, kissing her thoroughly until he felt her shudder in his arms. Or was that him?

Never had he longed like this for a woman. Never had he cared so deeply, wanted so badly, and it scared the shit out of him. He was usually all business, but she made him yearn for more—for family, friends, for the plain and simple goodness of love. Everything he thought would always be out of his reach.

"Maddie," he whispered as he fumbled with the tiny buttons on her blouse.

"What is it?" She was kissing him right back, meeting all his demands. Her hips pushed against him, her hands moved up and down his chest and tugged at his pants. Lord, the woman was driving him insane. Did she not know how close he was to the edge?

Nick had come clean about a lot of things, but there was just one more teensy-weensy thing he really had to mention. *The extra shares.* But Maddie jumped into his arms and wrapped those toned, tanned legs around him and, on a scale of one to ten, this little issue became a negative one hundred.

He pushed her against the Justin Timberlake poster on the door, cupped her gorgeous ass, and whispered every sweet thing he wanted to do to her, even as he swept aside the scrap of material she called a panty and claimed his prize.

His hands skimmed her hot liquid center, surprised and thrilled at how ready she was. For him. No one but him. The thought made him crazy with desire. He had to slow himself down so he could linger over the soft terrain of her curves, show her with soft kisses and his alleged legendary finesse just how much he ached for her, had to have her. She ran her hands up and down the muscles of his back, through his hair, over his crotch until he thought he was going to self-combust on the spot.

A low moan escaped his lips. He was never going to make it through foreplay.

Beads of sweat formed on his forehead, and he started to do ancient math problems to slow himself down. *What are the prime numbers? What's 246 divided by 3 then multiplied by two?* Like the businessman he was, his life was usually full of efficiency, of cutting to the chase. Except now he wanted to please her, to pull out the stops and give her the best damn lovemaking of her life.

She must have sensed his hesitation, the frisson between *I want to rip all your clothes off and take you right here* and *I want to savor you all night.*

"What is it?" she gasped, out of breath. Her cheeks were flushed with color, her hair was halfway out of her fancy do, and he'd never seen her more gorgeous. "Oh, my God. Is there someone else? Those women at the auction—the ones bidding—"

"No!" He couldn't get the word out fast enough. "There's no one. There's been no one since a year ago—since Atlanta."

"What?" Her hands stopped moving, and she sidled out of his arms to stand and stare at him, her eyes big and wide. "No one since—me?"

He shrugged. "Ever since then, I've been…restless. No one's interested me enough. When I first saw you at the auction, I actually thought you'd come there because you wanted me."

"I did want you," Maddie said softly. "In more ways than I realized."

She'd taken a huge gamble on him, believing that bringing him here would save her company. Little did she know she'd saved him as well.

Without another word, she lifted herself on tiptoe to plant a soft kiss on his lips that was so soft, so sweet, he felt his heart would burst from the sheer joy of it. He wanted with every fiber of his being to deserve her, to be the man she believed he was.

He'd pulled back a bit without realizing it. "I—I need to slow down or else—"

"No," she said firmly. "No slowing down." She finished unbuttoning his shirt and tossed it to the floor.

"It won't be good for you."

"It'll be good." She smiled a knowing smile, steering him directly to the bed. Shedding her skirt, she kissed him thoroughly with wet, deep kisses that made his head reel. The pressure of her warm, soft breasts pushing into him made him groan out loud. "Oh, God, Maddie. I want you so bad, I—"

"Sh," she said, tugging at his belt.

Her blouse joined his shirt on the floor. She turned so he could unhitch her bra and add it to the growing pile of clothes, then he spun her back around. He admired the rounded globes of her breasts before taking each one up gently in his hands. He carefully smoothed his thumbs over the perfect pink tips, rubbed them slowly between his thumb and forefinger until she arched toward him and whispered his name on a raw sigh.

He placed a nipple in his mouth, flicking it lightly with his tongue until it hardened. She let loose a hunger-driven moan and grabbed his cock. She circled her thumb on the tip then grasped his shaft until it was his turn to moan.

He couldn't take anymore. With one swift motion, he tossed her onto the frilly pink bedspread and peeled off her panties. Making quick work of his pants and briefs, he settled his weight on top of her, his bare chest skimming her beautiful breasts.

He sank his hands into her thick, tumbling hair and cradled her face. She was looking at him like no one had ever looked at him before, without judgment, but with hunger that matched his own. He was compelled to speak, and when he did, his voice came out low and gravelly. "Nothing's been the same since last year. All I can think about is wanting you."

• • •

Maddie swallowed hard. "You—you've wanted me since last year?"

"No, not really." He reached two fingers up to smooth out the frown lines between her brows and grinned. "More like ten years. Make that forever."

Nick had taken advantage of her confusion to lift himself off her and spread her legs wide. Feather light kisses trailed up her thigh and kept going. She gasped as his tongue separated her most sensitive folds, traced along the vulnerable flesh, seared a path into her soul.

"Nick, Nick, I—"

"Sh." One of his fingers entered her, then another, his thumb stroking her core. Her legs quivered, and she clutched at his shoulders, as her head rolled back and forth on the pillow. Waves of warm sensation wafted over her, flowed through her, coiling a spring inside her tighter and tighter till she felt close and frantic. In desperation, she pulled him toward her.

"Now," she begged. "Please, now."

Somewhere far away she heard Hughie bark and a door close. Closer, the faint rip of a condom wrapper, then Nick was poised against her yielding flesh and pushing into her. There was no hesitation, no cautious inch-by-inch tiptoeing, but a quick hungry glide that filled her to her very core and made her gasp breathlessly as he possessed her utterly.

Higher and higher, their bodies sealed tightly together, Nick lifted her until she felt like her entire body was a bundle of rubber bands taut and ready to spring. His mouth possessed hers, and in between kisses he whispered sweet words. "I've never—felt—like this. Maddie, I—"

Maddie cried out his name, and he smothered the sound

with consuming, feverish kisses until his own breath came in soft, short gasps. His gaze locked with hers as they rode each wave together. She had never seen such tenderness in his warm brown eyes.

When it was over, he soothed her and stroked her and pulled her close to him. They lay there with her back tucked into his front, him biting her shoulder playfully. And it was the most perfect moment of her life.

"Nick," Maddie said after a long while.

"Mm," he responded, his voice far off and sleepy.

"You never asked me how many people I slept with in the past year."

He squeezed her arm where his was draped over hers. She heard him wince. He was definitely awake now. "Don't tell me," he said.

She turned to him. "Would you be jealous?"

"I don't want to think about it."

"Good. Because I didn't either. Sleep with anyone, that is."

"Why not?"

She reached up and lifted the tumble of hair off his forehead, ran the back of her hand down the sexy stubble of his cheek. The realization dawned on her halfway down his face, her fingers shaking as she touched his precious cheek.

She loved him.

She always had, but she didn't dare say it or he'd run from her faster than college kids in a middle-of-the-night dorm fire drill.

She was so screwed. He was good at avoiding messy entanglements, at cutting people off. He'd done it to her before when they were much younger, and even last year. So she pulled her hand away and smiled casually. "I can't explain it, really, just that it was like the Cinderella shoe."

"Our lovemaking was like a shoe?"

"We just...fit." Plain and simple. One man, one perfect fit.

She bit her lip. She'd said too much. He wasn't a sentimental man. She had a feeling it had cost him a lot to admit that he, the most notorious playboy in Philadelphia, had been celibate for a year. Because of her.

Nick raised himself up on an elbow, skimming his fingers lightly over her body, arousing goose bumps of sensation everywhere. All the while he gazed at her like she was a treasured work of art. Finally, the quirk of a smile lit on his lips. "I think we have some lost time to make up for, Madison Marie. And by the way, I agree with your assessment. We fit pretty damn fine."

. . .

2:00 a.m.

Nick glanced at the Winnie the Pooh light-up alarm clock on the bedside table. It cast a glow on the blush pink walls and illuminated the soft curve of Maddie's shoulder, the tumbled mass of her hair as she lay sleeping beside him in her girlish bed where they had done things that were decidedly not girlish. Maddie's head was tucked under his shoulder, his arm splayed around her waist, the rose-dotted sheet tangled somewhere around their legs.

His first impulse was to wake her, make love to her a third time, quench his unslakable thirst for her. Part of him didn't believe what had happened, that she'd fade away as quickly as dawn would creep into the dark room and blanch out memories of the night. He was used to that—no promises, no expectations, nothing at stake. But this weekend, everything was upside down. *He* was upside down. Leaving her felt wrong, and he feared this feeling of happiness would vanish forever as soon as he left the room.

He didn't want to go, but he didn't want to disrespect her mother and stay here all night, to appear in the hall in the morning yawning and puffing out his chest like some redneck guest. Not his style. Not to mention he had no desire to face Derrick's wrath.

Nick eased Maddie's head onto her pillow, climbed out of bed, and pulled the sheet over her. He kissed her cheek, murmured in her ear why he felt he should go. Half asleep, she made a weak protest, then curled her hand under her pillow and settled into a deep slumber.

Nick pulled on his pants and flung on his shirt, checked his pocket for his wallet. He remembered his phone in the mailbox, and cracked an involuntary smile. For the first time ever, he actually felt the relief of not being tethered to it, of not having his attention split a thousand electronic ways. He felt suddenly in-the-moment present, and there was nowhere else he'd rather be.

A warm sense of peace washed over him. It wasn't just that he was sexually sated. He'd left women plenty of times in the middle of the night and never felt this contentment, this feeling of...home. That was it. He felt like he *belonged* somewhere for the first time.

Could it be that he'd finally found someone who wanted him for who he was and not how many yachts he owned or big parties he threw or which celebrities he rubbed elbows with?

Whoa. Nick knew enough about himself not to let his emotions run away on him. Maddie was a great woman, but he was certain this crazy sense of elation was temporary.

She was the marry-me-and-have-a-bunch-of-babies kind of person, and he wasn't cut out for that. To this day, he could barely think about losing his parents and baby sister. It was so long ago, but the hurt and the cold, blank aloneness stayed forever. He couldn't even think of loving someone like that again and setting himself up for that kind of pain.

One look at Maddie stirred an irrational, hopeful feeling in his chest. She was radiant in the glow of the nightlight, her hair a curtain of silk that cascaded everywhere. He wanted to jump back in bed and inhale its flowery fragrance, feel it tickle against his chest as she slept, watch it drape her shoulders like some sensuous Godiva. He wanted to make love to her a hundred more times.

A thousand more.

There would be time for that soon.

Nick looked back one last time and silently opened the door to the hall. He hadn't gone more than four steps when the door at the other end of the hallway opened and Derrick stepped out.

Oh, shit.

Too late now. Nick walked forward, wondering if the excuse of making a sandwich in the middle of the night would sound as contrived as he thought.

Derrick's hair stood haphazardly on end as he stumbled down the corridor in a wrinkled T-shirt and striped pajama bottoms. He yawned widely, and Nick thought at first he hadn't seen him. It was dim, after all, one lamp lit on a table halfway down the hall.

Derrick flicked a switch. Wall sconces lit up the space with bright yellow light like an FBI interrogation room. He pinned Nick with his gaze. "What are you doing here?"

Nick kept his cool. "I could ask you the same question."

"One of the twins had too much ice cream at the festival today. Jenna sent me for clean clothes."

"Oh. Sorry, man."

"That's all right. Once you have kids you don't sleep much anyway." He waited for Nick to answer his question.

Nick took a big breath. "I was just looking for another blanket. The dog—um—sort of stole mine."

It was the truth. Yesterday's, but the truth.

"The linen closet is that way." Derrick pointed a thumb behind his head.

"Thanks. Good luck." Nick walked past him, and opened the linen closet door.

"Tell Hughie to share. Oh, and Nick." Derrick spun around to face him. Sharp eyes bore down, and threat was written all over his face. Nick wasn't sure if he should toss his arms up in surrender or brace for a fight. "If you hurt my sister, I'll tear your heart out."

"Right. Got it." When Nick looked up, Derrick was halfway down the hall, not bothering to wait for his answer.

Nick pulled out a plaid wool blanket and walked downstairs to the darkened family room. Hughie was sprawled on the couch with his legs high in the air, softly snoring. "Move over, buddy," he said, nudging the dog aside.

Hugh snorted and rolled over, poking his big snout into Nick's hands to demand a pet, licking them and getting ready to snuggle up. Nick scratched his ears, patted his massive back. "You're not what I had in mind for tonight, Hugh boy, but you'll have to do."

Hughie turned on his back and used doggie body language to show he wanted his tummy rubbed.

Nick indulged the dog for a few minutes, then pulled a pillow off the back of the couch and laid down, tossing the blanket over both of them.

Chapter Eighteen

Birds chirped and warbled, a riot of birdie gossip right outside Maddie's window that awakened her from a deep slumber. She pried open an eye to find her familiar old room coated in the gray light of an early summer dawn.

Nick. Her blank slate of half-awakeness chalked up fast. She did a search mission with her arm around the rest of the bed, hoping he'd still be there.

Panic led her back to that night last year when she awakened to an empty bed. She knew he feared commitment, didn't take emotional risks. But hadn't he confessed their meeting in Atlanta was no accident? And that he hadn't been with anybody since?

Last night he'd held her, whispered her name, like she was cherished and beloved. He'd looked at her like he knew exactly who she was. Like he *got* her like no one ever had before. She refused to let doubts creep in.

She would not allow the old family trouble to drive a

wedge between them again. Today at the meeting she would announce her idea to work with Nick's grandfather. Nick would be pleased. After all, he'd believed in and supported her from the get-go.

Once Samuel saw her drawings, she had every hope he'd be eager to work with her to get their designs in front of a real audience. The company would be improved and united, and their problems would be over. Then her life with Nick could finally start.

For the first time, she felt freedom to make her own choices, to love whom she wanted. To bring her ideas into the company, to give it a new injection of creativity—to take it in a direction *she* would define. The possibilities thrilled her.

She needed to find Nick, tell him that she didn't want to waste another minute without him.

The sweet, pure realization made her clutch the back of her door for balance. Justin Timberlake looked at her, his expression baleful and smoldering. *Are you sure you want to give me up for him?* his youthful face seemed to ask.

She'd never been more certain.

Maddie pulled a T-shirt and girl boxers from her suitcase and yanked on her robe. She pulled open the door and gasped, slapping her hands over her mouth to stifle a scream. Cat stood in the hall, her hand poised to knock. She wore a ratty pink bathrobe and her pretty blond curls were mussed, making Maddie recall pictures of the two of them from a childhood Christmas morning when they were toddlers. Except Cat's eyes were puffy and swollen and she clutched a wad of Kleenex in one hand.

Maddie pulled her sister into her room and quietly shut

the door. "What's wrong?"

She knew the way her gut clenched that this was not something fixable, like a lost Barbie or a mean girl at school who made fun of Cat's thick glasses or a boy who didn't call. Those were things a big sister could fix with ice cream or a hot new CD or a few words of reassurance.

"Robert left. For good." Tears streamed down Cat's cheeks and her nose ran. Maddie steered her to the bed and propped up pillows behind her head.

"Oh, honey." She touched her sister's cheek, rubbed her arm, handed her more Kleenex from the bathroom.

"He said he was un-unhappy." She hiccupped through tears.

"What was there to be unhappy about? You're smart, ambitious, beautiful…"

A sudden sinking feeling made Maddie collapse onto her bed. "Oh, Cat. The money." Waves of nausea struck and her gut twisted like a wrung-out rag. She thought back to the night of the auction. She'd turned to her sister impulsively, because she knew her sister would never let her down. Cat was one hundred percent loyal.

"This is my fault." She wanted to tell Cat she'd replace the money immediately, but that would be a lie. She was weeks, if not months, away from a real paycheck.

"I gave it to you because you're my sister," Cat said. "You were only out to help Dad."

Maddie had been out to save the company, but she couldn't help wonder if some secretive, subconscious part of her had wanted Nick for completely different reasons.

She gripped her sister by the shoulders. She hated the idea of having a calculating, anal penny-pincher for a brother-in-law, but it wasn't her choice to make. "Robert had a right to be angry about the money. I should never have asked you to bail me out like that."

"That's not the only reason he left."

Maddie frowned.

"He couldn't handle the chaos. The kids running around, you and Nick covered with pie, Grandmeel's horrible confession. He said he calculated our risk of future unhappiness and it was way too high. And…there's more."

"More?"

"It's…a little sexual."

Oh God. Did he construct algorithms in bed? Did Maddie really want to know?

"He didn't like…what I mean is, he didn't want to…" Her face was red and she was stammering. "Let's just say the one number he didn't like was sixty-nine."

Maddie blew out a breath of relief. That regimented bastard had really done a number on her. "Oh, Cat. It's good he's gone. Normal guys love sixty-nine."

"I thought I wanted predictable, you know?"

Oh, Maddie knew. Safe. Orderly. Not dangerous. Like Cat's longtime crush Preston Guthrie, Derrick's longtime best friend and Nick's business partner, whom she'd finally managed to get over. Ever since Cat suffered from horrendous asthma as a child, they'd all watched over her, tried to keep her safe and protected. But Preston had appealed disastrously to her very hidden wild side.

Cat dissolved into tears again.

"Whatever happened, you're a wonderful sister, and I don't deserve you." She squeezed Cat tightly, like she'd done often when they were small children and she'd been overcome with the need to keep her safe. "I'll make us some coffee, okay? Then we'll talk."

Cat nodded helplessly as Maddie went into big sister mode, plumping pillows and handing her more Kleenex. Too bad the real fix was much more complicated.

Maddie padded into the kitchen, where she quickly started the coffee, trying to be as quiet as possible. One glance over at the couch showed a big hairy lump covered with a blanket that was most certainly not Nick. Once the coffee pot started trickling, she went to have a better look.

Hughie was sprawled in all his glory over nearly the entire couch. The soft woolen blanket was tucked in under his chin. Nick lay with eyes closed on the floor, propped on his side against the couch with arms crossed in front of him. Hughie snorted, suddenly awake, and looked expectantly at Maddie. His tail began to pound thunderously against the leather cushions.

"Hughie! Off the couch!" Maddie said. Hughie's ears drooped and he slunk off, gingerly stepping around Nick's sleeping form. Maddie knelt down beside Nick, ruffled his messy hair, and kissed him on the forehead. "You should have stayed in my bed."

Nick's eyes opened, and his mouth tipped up in a slow grin. His already thick six a.m. stubble looked incredibly sexy. "Is that an invitation?" He looked around the dim room. "Because it looks like we still may have time for…"

Just then Alex and Logan came tearing into the room yelling and laughing and hurled themselves on Nick. Maddie plucked them off, but they toppled right back onto Nick like magnets, unable to stay away. "Quiet, guys, you'll wake Grandma."

"What are you two doing up so early?" Nick didn't sound the least bit fazed that two little boys were sitting on him at six o'clock in the morning.

"Time for Power Rangers," Alex said. He bounced up and down on Nick's chest. His pajama bottoms displayed action heroes in primary colors jumping, leaping, and looking bad-assed.

"We watch them every morning. Will you get us breakfast, Aunt Maddie?" Logan asked.

Great. They were already separating along gender lines, looking to Nick for horsing-around-guy stuff and Maddie for supplying food.

"How about some dry cereal?" Nick asked. "I'll get it."

"Stay here and play." Maddie got up to tend to the coffee. Alex handled the remote with skills better than most adults and found the correct channel. The boys spring boarded from Nick onto the couch and settled in.

"Uncle Nick, come watch with us." Alex tugged on Nick's T-shirt.

"Yeah, come watch." Logan patted the couch next to him.

Hughie decided to accept the invitation for himself, hopping up and settling in.

Maddie saw the expression on Nick's face morph from amusement to something deeper—a vulnerability she'd never seen. Like the lone kid on the playground who suddenly gets accepted into the group.

"Save me a seat, guys. I'll get us some cereal."

Nick got up and walked into the kitchen. "Hey there, beautiful." Maddie felt his smile all the way down to her toes and in some other places, too.

As he reached above her head for a coffee mug, he kissed her forehead. His arm curled around her waist, and the tension inside her eased a little. "Thanks for the coffee," he said. "Hey, I need to talk to you. After Power Rangers?"

Maddie froze in the middle of pouring Cat's coffee. When guys wanted to talk after sex, it was never good. She searched his eyes for reassurance. "Should I worry?"

He met her gaze head on, but didn't look as untroubled as she'd hoped. If he wasn't always so calm and confident, she'd even peg him as nervous. Her heart somersaulted. "What is it?" Her own voice sounded foreign.

He set down the coffee and took up her hands in his big ones, smoothed her fingers with his thumbs. His warm, gentle touch soothed her. "Nothing to worry about. I just want to talk to you before the meeting today." He pulled her hands to his lips and kissed her knuckles. "Maddie, last night was — "

"Hurry up, Uncle Nick. You're missing the giant monster with nine heads."

"—incredible," he said, and Maddie's heart gave an expectant leap. "I want you to know that."

"I needed to hear that right now," Maddie said. "Cat's in my room. Robert left. I think for good."

"I can't say I'm surprised. Did she say why?"

Maddie's stomach churned and it wasn't from the strong coffee. "Cat said something about risk calculation, but I'm worried about something I might have done."

"I know about the loan. Robert told me last night. If it makes you feel any better, I think there were some other issues going on between them."

"I put her in a bad position."

"I agree it wasn't the best choice, but Robert is wealthy enough that making a contribution to a children's hospital isn't going to break him. Besides, if you hadn't made the bet, I wouldn't be here." He bent and kissed her. "Is there anything I can do?"

Maddie nodded toward the boys. "Being with them is a good idea."

"Happy to. I've got plenty of time before I pick my granddad up for breakfast. Is something else wrong? You look worried."

Yeah, she was worried. He was his usual charming self but what was going through his head that he wanted to talk about? The business agreement between their families wasn't sealed. Maybe he was having second thoughts. Worse, maybe he was having second thoughts about *her*. She'd thought they'd broken through a huge barrier last night but maybe she was wrong.

"You're going to do great today." He reached out to massage the worry lines between her eyes. Then he tapped her on the chest. "When in doubt, follow this."

She already had followed her heart, and it had led her straight to him. Still, she couldn't shake the unsettled feeling that the perfect day wasn't going to be so perfect after all.

Chapter Nineteen

"Okay, we're all set up." Maddie looked around the board-room and smiled that sweet, open smile Nick had come to love. There was something fragile about her that she hid well, despite her polished look in a black suit and heels and confident carriage. He knew how important this meeting was to her, how much she had riding on it.

"You'll do great." He saw the stress in her face, the faint traces of self-doubt that remained. The morning had got away from him. She'd been occupied with her sister and he'd left for breakfast with Gramps. He still hadn't mentioned the shares.

Now, Nick. It's your last chance.

"Maddie, I have to tell you something."

Color rose in her cheeks. Her trusting smile twisted his guts. He didn't make a point of lying, even if this was a lie of omission. He opened his mouth to speak but her entire family piled into the conference room, laughing and chatting, and took their places around the big mahogany table, where a box sat covered with a pink satin drape.

Derrick and Jenna and Maddie's mother all sat. Cat was on a phone call, they explained, but would be here any second. Even Grandmeel came, dressed for Sunday church and looking nonplussed from last night's scene. Only Maddie's dad was missing, but that was because Maddie wanted to be certain all would go well before she laid out her plans to him.

"This is so exciting," Rosalyn said. She took a picture on her phone of Maddie standing at the front of the conference room to send to Maddie's father.

"Knock 'em dead, sis." Derrick gave a thumbs-up sign and grinned.

"Isn't Al coming?" Grandmeel asked suspiciously.

"He's on his annual fishing trip in Canada and his flight got delayed, so he won't be in until tonight," Maddie said. "He's given me his go-ahead, though."

Cat approached Maddie, holding her cell phone against her chest. "The press is waiting outside. Apparently Bob Russland from the Buckleberry Gazette saw all the commotion over here on a Sunday morning and wondered what's going on. He's asking if you'd make a statement for tomorrow's paper."

"It's too early for that, Cat," Maddie said. "We're just presenting ideas. Ultimately, we'll need Dad's approval."

"I'll try to hold him off, but you know how he is. Once he gets his hooks in a story, there's no resting until it's complete."

"I won't talk to anyone until Dad okays this plan. Besides, Uncle Al still has to go over some numbers with me."

"Okay, Maddie. You're the boss."

Nick felt the crick in his neck ease up a little. With the CFO gone, no one would be crunching numbers today. Hell, he might even be able to get rid of those extra shares by tomorrow, sign them over to Maddie as proof of his good intentions.

From the far end of the gleaming conference table, amid the ever-present smell of leather and shoe polish, he watched Maddie's presentation. She was feisty and animated and funny. She formally introduced his grandfather, and did it with grace and pride. "Samuel actually invented our patented orthopedic sole, and he's spent the last two decades designing newer generations of it that are more cushioned, more comfortable, and, most amazing of all...designed for a high heel."

The women around the table gasped.

"Here's our current line-up of sturdy, dependable shoes." A PowerPoint slide demonstrated the old tried-and-true models. "Cat, Jenna, do you own any of these?"

"I—er—I used to," Cat said.

"Right. When you were twelve. I know because we both had the same pair."

Jenna shook her head. "I can't say I do, but I bought my grandma a pair and she loves them."

"We want to keep the sturdy and dependable part and couple it with cute and gotta-have-it style." She clicked the remote and the screen lit up with numerous shoes in bright colors. "Imagine flats in all colors and geometrics that support and cushion your foot so you can walk in them all day and still feel energized." She clicked again. "Imagine heels that are actually comfortable. And baby-boomer shoes for people with foot issues in bright, vivid colors, not just white and beige and black. And lastly, imagine this."

Maddie nodded to Samuel, who pulled back his chair and walked to the front of the table where he pulled off the pink silk cover. "This," she said, "is the prototype of a shoe. I drew it, and Samuel did a quick mock-up for today. We call it *The Cinderella*."

It was stunning, with lace and crystals, a silver platform, and a five-inch silver heel. As impractical and non-orthopedic as they came.

"We want to design this with our trademark sole. Samuel thinks it can be done. And we're going to enter it in the Bergdorf shoe competition."

Nick raised his brows. Innovative, stylish. Clever. Pride pulsed through him. Maddie deserved this. She'd worked hard for it. Her ideas were smart and forward-thinking.

His grandfather stood quietly beside Maddie, beaming. Nick had never seen him so proud or happy, except maybe on the day Nick had graduated from college.

"It's ergonomically designed not to fatigue your foot. To take the pressure off the tarsal bones," Samuel said. He sounded like a kid ordering from the ice cream truck.

Maddie's mother raised her hand and spoke. "Maddie, this is all wonderful but I don't want your father coming back to learn the whole company has changed. We've kept so much from him. I—I just don't feel honest not having him here."

"Daddy's still the majority owner, Mom. We'd never proceed without him."

Nick shifted in his seat. Everything was going well, so now was not the time to correct the misconception.

"That's not exactly true, Madison." A big voice boomed into the room. Everyone turned to watch a large, imposing man walk into the room, a cup of steaming black coffee in his hand. He wore khaki shorts and a fishing hat covered with lures. *Uncle Al.* Nick felt the hair at the back of his neck bristle. He sat up straight in his chair.

"Your new majority owner is sitting right here at the table. The wolf among sheep, so to speak. Morning, Mr. Holter. I'm Al Watson."

Nick drew in a sharp breath and went into damage control mode.

Maddie broke the shocked silence. "Uncle Al, what are you talking about? Of course Dad is still the majority owner."

"I'm surprised your boyfriend didn't tell you, Maddie. Holter Enterprises has owned over fifty percent of our shares for some time now. Fifty-two percent, to be exact."

Her shocked expression made Nick cringe. "It's not what you think," he said quickly.

"That's impossible," Maddie said. She faced her uncle, still standing straight, still in command. "You told me last month only forty-two percent went up for sale. Nick, set him straight. Tell him the truth." Maddie turned to him, shaken. She'd gone stark white. "Please."

That one syllable gutted him worse than a knife. It showed him she knew. She was still hoping against hope, but she'd figured it out.

He'd lied.

"Let me explain."

"There's not much explaining to do, boy." Al tapped his meaty hands on the fine old table and addressed the family. "We put a few of your father's shares up for sale a year or so ago and they were bought immediately by Viper Enterprises. I didn't realize until this morning that Viper was you, Mr. Holter."

"Viper Enterprises? What's that?" Rosalyn asked.

Nick answered. "One of my investment firms. Look, it was no secret I was originally looking to acquire the company, but all that's changed now." He took a step toward Maddie, but she backed away.

"When were you going to tell me that Kingston Shoes is now *Holter* Shoes?" she asked.

Nick scrubbed a hand over his face. Pairs of eyes stabbed glares at him. There was no rule in his arsenal to fall back on. All he knew was he had to make her understand, make her see.

"I tried several times, but either you were so excited about your plans, or upset about your dad, and then this morning was crazy and I just…I couldn't tell you." He tried to approach her again.

She shook her head. "Please. Don't."

Excuses. He was making them to them and to himself. He hadn't told her because he hadn't *wanted* to tell her. The Kingston name was important and now it was technically owned by the enemy.

"Look, I thought about dumping the extra shares, but then I figured it would be protective if I held onto them. In case your plans faltered, you'd have an ally controlling the cards, someone to help you out behind the scenes if you weren't able to resuscitate the company by yourself."

Maddie's eyes went wide. "So you were going to make it impossible for me to fail?"

"No—all right, yes. You know I came here with every intention of taking over, but everything's different now."

"Good Lord. He meant all along to dissolve us," Grandmeel exclaimed, fueling the fire.

"He's keeping the company intact, Gran. Let the man talk." Derrick shut her down immediately, and for once Nick was grateful for his bluntness.

"It was clear to me early on that if I didn't buy the stock someone else would. So I bought it. All of it. At first it was for me—I had your company in my hands to do with what I wanted. To bring justice to my grandfather. But that reason no longer exists."

"No." Maddie whirled toward her brother. "Grandmeel is right. Kingston Shoes is no longer owned by Kingstons. I sort of consider that dissolved."

Maddie left the front of the room to stand before Nick. "I suppose I should thank you for saving everyone's jobs. You even saved mine. What were you going to do, inject some cash secretly to make it look like I was succeeding?"

"Actually, Holter Enterprises just infused half a million dollars into the company as of yesterday," Al said.

Maddie cast him a horrified look. How could his good intentions turn out so badly? "For God's sakes, Maddie, I was trying to protect you."

"I don't want your protection," she said. "I thought you believed in me when no one else did. I thought you *got* me. But Nick Holter's always got to be in charge, in control. Except you lied to me, Nick, and lying isn't right. Not with someone you trust. You're exactly what they say—a shark."

"It's not like that. I don't care about revenge anymore, and I don't want your company. I—I've changed, Maddie, because of you. What else do you want from me?"

"How about the truth? You have the power and money to manipulate everything and everyone to your own satisfaction. But now you're lying to yourself. You got exactly what you wanted—our company in your hands. You won." She looked shocked, pale, defeated. "I want you to go. Now. Please leave us alone." She turned to the window and folded her arms.

Her family just sat, saying nothing. Nick touched her arm, but she shrugged him away. "Please go," she said.

Derrick's chair scraped, and he headed in their direction. Nick was about to be bounced out.

"I'm sorry, Maddie," Nick said to her back. Then he walked out the door.

• • •

"Maddie, are you saying Nick didn't come here to help us?" her mother asked.

"He came because I bought him in an auction. An auction for rich people. I took Cat's wedding money for it and now Robert's gone. I've lost the company. Worse, I knew what Nick was planning all along and didn't say anything. I thought I could handle it myself and convince him otherwise. I'm sorry."

Silence hummed and crackled as everyone shifted uncomfortably in their seats.

Finally, Samuel cleared his throat. "I want you all to know that I have no interest in running anything. I'm delighted for the opportunity to work with Maddie and I sincerely hope that we still can."

Derrick tapped his fingers on the shiny table. "But your grandson just bought our company out from beneath us. He's in charge now."

Maddie nodded. "He can do whatever he wants, run the company the way he pleases. He's the majority owner." She thought of her father. How could she tell him?

"I hate to say this, but this is what happens when you bed the enemy," Grandmeel said. "They sneak up on you when you're not looking and bam! Everything's lost."

"Amelia, that's quite enough," Maddie's mother said.

Maddie whirled to face her grandmother. She bit back tears and bitter disappointment, promising to give into them later, in private. "Maybe I am a screw-up. Maybe Nick bought us up without my knowing. Maybe I lost the company for good. But you know what, Grandmeel? You are by far the worst excuse for a grandmother I have ever seen. You are mean and spiteful and—and just plain nasty and I am tired of pretending you're not."

Amelia's jaw dropped. Cat, Jenna, and Maddie's mother cast Maddie sympathetic looks, Samuel shifted in his seat, Al shook his head sadly, and Derrick—well, God only knew what he was thinking. But for the first time, Maddie didn't care.

"Well, I never—" her grandmother exclaimed in typical drama queen fashion.

Maddie didn't wait to hear the rest. She picked up her portfolio and left the room, ran down the stairs and out of the building. Right into the arms of a camera crew from local WKAP.

"Is there a change in ownership of Kingston Shoes?"

"Is your father too infirm to ever return?"

"Will people lose their jobs?"

Maddie put her hands up to shelter her face from the flashing bulbs. How the hell did a small town get so many cameras? "I—I'm sorry. No comment." Maddie dodged the shouted questions buffeting her from all sides. Bob Russland from the Gazette was one of her classmates from high school. He approached her, thrusting a microphone in her face. So much for schoolmate loyalty.

She had a vague memory of the night of the auction, the last time she'd spoken in front of a crowd. She'd been flirtatious and witty, and clueless. Light years away. Biting her cheeks to hold back tears, she pushed her way to the sidewalk. She could barely breathe. Grief and shame filled her chest, and her legs felt numb and limp as jelly.

She wanted to take off down the street, crawl into her bed and hide.

A voice mocked inside her head. *Flighty Maddie. A screw up despite her best intentions.*

She looked past the reporters. Folks had gathered because of the commotion, some on their way out of church and heading to Ida's for pancake brunch. She recognized Patsy Yates from the Five and Dime and Reverend Fletcher himself, fresh from his sermon. Was he wondering why her entire family had skipped service today?

Suddenly, Maddie stopped. She was not going to run away. Somehow she would summon the strength to stay. She owed that much to all the townspeople who were worried about their jobs at the company. She took a big breath and forced a smile. Then she turned and spoke into the microphone. "Kingston Shoes is undergoing a big, bold revolution that will ensure that everyone—one hundred percent everyone—will keep their jobs. My father is steadily recovering, and until he's back, I will be taking the helm. I'm bringing in new designs for brand new shoe styles. But that doesn't mean we'll stop manufacturing our tried and true shoes. Overall, Kingston Shoes will be back, bigger and better than ever."

She made eye contact although it took every shred of will to hold up her head. She smiled, even though her heart was broken. She even shook Russ's hand when he thanked her for the inspiring words she'd spoken.

At last, video equipment was hoisted off shoulders, and the press slowly dispersed. Maddie walked down Main Street, past the familiar shops, the flower pots, the fire hydrants painted bright neon shades, the diagonal yellow strips on Main Street for parked cars. The big banner left from the Berry Festival looked forlorn, one end detached and hanging limply. The park was empty of booths, and the grass was downtrodden from all the foot traffic. A lone sign announced the fireworks display at dusk tonight. Another Berry Festival had come and gone. The weekend was nearly over.

The turn came up to head home, but she continued walking straight ahead. She'd rallied the courage to tell the town what she had to tell them. Everything else, on the other hand, was a total mess. The company was out of her family's control, and it had been all along. She'd strong-armed her sister out of her honeymoon money and she'd told her grandmother off for the first time.

Worse, she *had* slept with the enemy, and she'd allowed him to break her heart. Again.

Chapter Twenty

Maddie found her father sitting in the rehab hospital garden reading the *Buckleberry Gazette*, his wheelchair beneath a live oak dripping with moss. She wished that wise, ancient tree could wrap its sprawling arms around her, and protect her and her dad from the pain she was about to inflict.

"Hey, Sugar," her dad said, taking off his reading glasses. That same twinkle that always shone in his eyes was back. It was a sign of her dad before the stroke, and it shot a brief wave of relief through her.

She'd do anything to spare him bad news. The irony was she'd done the exact same thing to her dad as Nick had done to her—not telling him things, keeping him out of the loop. Her dad deserved better than that, and now she had to come clean.

Maddie kissed him and sat on a bright green park bench. Lush impatiens bloomed in pinks and reds and whites, and a border of monkey grass lined a tall, splashing fountain.

Despite the shade, sweat collected beneath her suit jacket, and she shrugged it off. "Aren't you hot?" she asked hopefully. "We could go in." That would delay her dreaded announcement at least another five minutes.

"I've missed the sunshine." Her dad neatly folded his paper into quarters and assessed his daughter with that quiet look he'd given her many times. Even when she was in hot water as a kid, he'd always waited her out, let her say her piece.

Where to even start? Maddie did the only thing she knew, took a deep breath and plunged in.

"Daddy." She took up both her father's hands and looked him straight in the eye. "So many things have been going on that I haven't told you about. Nick's owned more than half our company all along. It happened right under my nose, and I'm so sorry."

Maddie heaved a sob. She put her head in her hands. Her father placed his hand on her head and patted it. How many times had he done this during the storms of her childhood? But she wasn't a child. She was an adult in charge of big decisions that could make or break a company.

"You were always kindhearted even as a little girl, Madison," he said. "You always took other people's suffering personally. But sometimes there's only so much you can do, despite the best intentions."

Madison eyeballed her father through a blur of tears. He seemed awfully calm for what she'd just told him. "What are you saying, Daddy?"

"Nick's already been here. He told me what's been going on."

She could only imagine. "What did he say?"

"He told me how he came to buy up the shares, and how he wanted the company to make up for the injustices done to his grandfather. But he no longer wants revenge. Said that changed because of you."

"I know he saved our company and all the jobs, but he never told me about owning most of our shares. He even infused a bunch of cash so it would look like I succeeded. I don't need a billionaire to set me up in a foolproof situation."

She paused and braced herself, expecting a lecture about being grateful to an enormously powerful man who'd rushed in and saved the day. Hell, maybe she *should* be grateful, but she was too damn independent to expect someone to save her. She wanted the chance to save that company herself, with her own brains and hard work.

"I agree," her father said.

"What?" Her mouth fell open.

"I agree you don't need Nicholas to ensure your success. From what he told me, you're well on your way to doing that all by yourself. I'm so proud of you, Madison."

"You're proud of me?"

"I've always been proud of you. You've always been harder on yourself than anyone else ever has."

"That doesn't excuse my screw-ups, Dad."

"Honey, life doesn't come with an instruction manual. Sometimes that's how we figure out what we want—by figuring out what we *don't* want. You've always had the courage to go out and take chances."

Yes, and her chance-taking had mostly led to disaster. "I've had plenty of practice with that."

"Trouble is, I think you'd do anything to help us at the expense of your own happiness. I don't want you to carry this burden by yourself anymore. Maybe it would be best for us to sell off the whole company to Nick. Then you could get your job in Philly back. I was wrong to try and tie you down to something you don't want."

"I know where I belong now, and it's here." She grasped her father's hand. "I have a plan, Daddy. A plan for Kingston Shoes that might just bring us back better than ever." Maybe she didn't have a business degree, but what she did have was artistic sense, gut instincts. And, most important of all, she *loved* shoes.

"You're a loyal daughter, Madison, and I love you. Dearly."

"Oh, Daddy." Tears plopped ungraciously down her cheeks. "I love you, too. So much."

As they embraced in the shade of that old oak, Maddie knew she'd made one right decision. She would do everything in her power to bring their company back.

Her dad sat back in his chair and gripped her arm. "You know, Nick said we could buy our shares back whenever it's convenient. And he doesn't want to change the Kingston name."

Oh, God. Nick had restored the company to her family without wanting anything in return? Kingston Shoes was still Kingston Shoes. Relief washed through her, but it was temporary. Maddie squeezed her eyes shut as she remembered her hurtful words in the conference room. "I accused Nick of wanting the company for himself. But all he really wants is for me to find a place for his grandfather." She hadn't agreed with his methods, but she couldn't argue about everything he'd done for them.

Her father's mouth was tilted up in the slightest smile.

"He's a good man, Maddie. Even the best shoes need some adjusting now and again."

"I love him, Dad. I think I always have."

"Then you'd best catch him before he leaves."

She shot her father a look of confusion.

"He told me he had to get back to Philadelphia and that his private pilot was meeting him at the airport. Said he was catching a cab downtown and he'd arrange for someone to pick up the rental car in a day or two."

Two blocks away. A minute if she ran. Maddie kissed her father. "Dad, I've got to go."

• • •

"Nick, wait," Maddie called just as a yellow cab pulled to a stop in front of the coffee shop. Nick, his hand on the door handle, looked up.

He forced himself not to react to the panicked sound of her voice. She'd chosen not to believe him, thought he was out to take the company for himself even after all that had happened between them. This was the price he paid for exposing himself—his real self—to a woman. And it was a mistake he'd never make again.

He told the cabbie to wait and walked over to her. The cab sat idling, the faint smell of gasoline thick in the heavy air.

"My father told me what you did," she said. "That you'll let us buy back the shares, that you don't want the company."

"Maddie, I haven't wanted the company since I found out your father was sick." Not true. From the moment he'd laid eyes on her vamping it up at that stupid auction, his heart had been struck, and all his plans to avenge his grandfather had withered like a day-old balloon.

"Don't go."

He steeled himself against the pain that threatened to take him down. "The weekend's up, and I'm way behind on my work."

"Your work. Of course."

"I trust you'll watch out for my grandfather."

"That goes without saying," she said.

"I've got to go," he said without looking in her eyes because if he did, God only knew what would happen. "My pilot's picking me up in Charlotte."

"But you don't have your stuff."

"I'll send for it."

She tugged at his sleeve. "Can't we talk about this?"

Her hand burned, but he forced himself to shrug it off. "You've already pegged me as the bad guy. I don't see me changing that."

"I understand how much you've done, and I'm so, so grateful. But I confided in you. You knew how badly I wanted to turn things around. Going behind my back and arranging everything makes me feel like you had no belief in me at all."

Anger crashed against him in cold, hard waves. He felt stripped naked, wholly exposed. "Maddie, I did believe in you. I invested money because that's what I do. I put capital in companies that can make money, and all my instincts tell me you're going to do great things here. Too bad you can't see that." He headed toward the car.

"Just like that?" Her words stopped him. The muscles in his back and in his fists bunched. "You left in high school because you thought it had to be either me or your career. And you left last year because you felt guilty about your grandfather, but it wasn't really that, was it? Those were just excuses."

"What are you talking about?"

She stalked up to him and jabbed him in the chest. "You never let yourself get too close, do you? When it gets dangerous or hard, you convince yourself it's not worth it and run like the wind."

"I did my best to do the right thing, but it's not good enough for you. You still suspect my motives, like I'm a Holter and my ownership is soiling your company's name. Who's not trusting whom, Madison?"

Her blue eyes flashed with fury and confusion, and not a trace of sorrow or apology. The two of them could not be more opposed. North Pole and South. Red Sox and Yankees. Pepsi and Coke.

Nick paced the sidewalk. "And one more thing. You accuse me of not believing in you, but maybe the real problem is that you don't believe in yourself. Just once I wish you'd say to hell with what everyone thinks about your past and do the job you came to do."

Her mouth dropped open. That was a direct hit and for once she found no words to retaliate against his hurtful remarks.

Nick checked his watch. "I've got to go. Best of luck, Maddie."

He looked up to see her eyes filling with tears for the first time that day. Oh, hell, what a mess he'd made. As he climbed into the cab, he clenched his jaw tight to combat the impulse to look back, kept his gaze focused straight ahead as they puttered down Main Street, past the skewed Berry Festival banner and the ruined red, white, and blue streamers.

He should never have let her into his heart. He'd tried to help her the only way he knew how, doing the one thing he was good at: building companies. Backing her with support. But by rejecting his help, she'd rejected him.

People didn't have to die to leave you feeling alone, lost, and worse...betrayed. That was why he didn't do relationships. He'd broken his cardinal rule and fallen in love. Look where that had gotten him.

He reached for his cell and realized he didn't have it. God, he couldn't even do business. Tapping his fingers restlessly against the old leather seat, he squeezed his eyes shut and slumped down for a nap he knew he couldn't take, and left Buckleberry Bend far behind.

• • •

"What's wrong, Madison? Why did Nick just leave?" Cat asked.

Maddie swiped at her eyes. She forced a smile as Cat, Jenna, her mom, and the twins walked up to her as she stood on the sidewalk watching Nick's car disappear. Derrick pushed her dad in his wheelchair.

"Hey." She managed a weak smile. She hugged the twins, who had rushed up and tackled her at the knees.

Her mother scanned her face with that worried concern she saved for super serious times. "Oh, honey." She wrapped her arms around her daughter.

"You and Nick will work it out," her dad said.

"I'm not so sure, Dad, but I'm all right." She could curl up into a ball and cry her eyes out later. Starting now, she would make everyone believe she was competent enough to run this company. "Are you all on your way home for brunch?"

"Change of plans," Derrick said. "We're taking you to Ida's."

Eating her favorite blueberry pancakes right now was about as high on her list as gallbladder surgery, but the thought touched her.

"Thanks, but I've got to get working at the office."

"That's precisely why you need pancakes," Derrick said. "After lunch, we're all going to make you a real office next to Dad's. With a window and everything."

Maddie crossed her arms. "How do you all plan to do that, exactly? There's no room for another office."

"Oh, yes there is," Derrick said. "We're moving the break room to where the storage closet is. So you'd better pick out a wall color and fast. You can't do your job without a proper work space."

The twins clustered around her legs, looking up at her with big, round eyes. "Mommy said we could paint," Logan said.

"Daddy said I could pound nails!" Alex chimed in.

"And I'm going to hang curtains," Mom said.

"I'll set up your computer," Cat said.

"I'd like to go spend an hour or two at my desk getting some files ready for Maddie's first day tomorrow," her father said. "If they'll let me out today, that is."

"Um, I think you're out already, Dad," Cat said.

"Are you sure you're up to it, Henry?" Maddie's mom

asked.

"Only if you feed me pancakes first."

Cat gave Maddie a huge hug. Jenna did too, and Derrick was right behind her. Her crazy, imperfect family believed in her, rallied around her in her time of need. And she'd never loved them so much as she did right now.

Maddie glanced around at her family, noticing who was missing. "I really ticked Grandmeel off, didn't I?"

"But good," Derrick said, rubbing his cheek.

"She's off licking her wounds, but I believe this was a good wake up call for her," Maddie's mom said. "We've all done our share of not making waves with her over the years."

"I know it hasn't been easy, but you have always respected her," her dad said, maybe more to her mother than to Maddie.

"Until today," Maddie said.

Cat gave Maddie a squeeze. "Maybe it was time she finally got a clue how hurtful she can be sometimes."

"We all can be," Derrick said, stepping up and grabbing Maddie's hand. "I had a bad attitude, sis. I guess I felt like I wasn't doing enough and here you are leaving your job and your life to come here and help out the family. It was easy for me to call attention to your shortcomings to make myself look better. I'm sorry." A small smile turned up his mouth.

She hugged her brother. "You've found your life and your career, Derrick. For the first time, I finally feel like I've found mine."

Maddie ruffled the twins' hair and released the brake on her father's wheelchair for the walk to Ida's.

It was shaky, but she would have a fresh start. She'd have a chance to make her ideas shine.

Maddie wasn't the confused twenty-year-old who spent an extra year in college because she couldn't decide on a major, or the one who couldn't hold down a job, or the girl who almost married someone ridiculously, disastrously wrong for her.

She finally knew who she was. Despite her bone-deep sadness, she believed in herself and that she could power through with her plan. Now all she had to do was prove it. Who'd have thought she'd find herself a new life right here in Buckleberry Bend?

Even if the man she loved wouldn't be part of it.

Chapter Twenty-One

The company was boisterous, drinks flowed, and the prime rib was tender and exceptional. Or it would have been if all food didn't taste like sand. Nick's dinner companion was successful, poised, and beautiful. He'd gone out to a big, noisy benefit specifically so he could forget that the ceremony for the Bergdorf shoe competition was occurring tonight in New York, and his grandfather and Maddie were finalists.

"You should join us. We could win," Gramps had said.

"I'm in the middle of a huge deal for Children's Hospital, Gramps. It's been taking all my time."

"You're being stubborn. Maddie's doing an amazing job with the company. She's a great leader. And she got me a workroom, too. And a design team. I think she's going to accomplish great things."

Good for her. He knew she'd be fine with or without his help.

Nick took a sip of the seductively heady red Bordeaux,

not giving a rat's ass whether or not it slid down his throat in a burst of sumptuous flavor as the waiter had promised.

Berries. It tasted like berries.

A million memories flashed in his head like an old flickering movie. Maddie dressed up and sashaying onto that stage at the auction. In the boardroom, determined and resolute. In her childhood bedroom, her silky hair tumbling over him, brushing his chest while she stared at him with that clear, honest gaze. She had a habit of seeing deep inside of him, far beneath the ambitious businessman facade he'd created. She always saw the best in him. The man he could be. Hell, she saw the best in everybody.

It had been a long shot, but at that auction, Maddie had gambled everything on him. Not just money, but her whole self. And he'd let her down.

Well, hell, what more could he do to prove he believed in her? He'd left the company in her hands. This was what he got for violating his own principles. Of not keeping business and pleasure separate.

"You're not eating your dinner," a throaty voice chided.

Nick forced a smile and raised his glass again to his lips. Gayle Sommers was an attentive, attractive date, and he had no doubt how the evening would end if he wanted it to. "Just distracted by work."

"I can help you keep those distractions to a minimum," she whispered seductively, fingering her wine glass. She reached over the fine linen-clad table to lightly smooth her lovely hands over his. "You work too hard. You need a diversion."

"I took a long weekend earlier this summer."

"Oh, that little getaway to your home town? By the

way, I saw the write-ups in the paper last Sunday on all the bachelors. Did you really judge a pie contest?" She fished out her iPad, tapped it a few times, and handed him the electronic article.

Gayle looked a little horrified, like judging a pie contest was an activity far below her usual standards. But Nick just grinned. The headline read, *Billionaire Bachelor Visits Home Town, Matches 15K Donation for Children's Hospital.* There he was, surrounded by pies, holding a blue ribbon in his hand. Maddie stood off to the side, smiling. Little did they know they'd soon be wearing those beautiful pies instead of judging them.

The memory of licking the whipped cream from Maddie's neck filled him a warm thrill, but then he looked closer. On the wrist of the hand holding up the ribbon, clearly visible in the photo, was the braided bracelet Maddie and the twins had made. That tiny bracelet made of patriotic thread she'd given him now seemed to mean more to him than his Rolex.

An unexpected anguish hit him like a violent gut cramp in the middle of a great run. Suddenly, he wasn't grinning anymore. He bent his head to peruse the article. *Small businesses are the heart of America*, it began. How many of those small businesses had he dissolved without forethought, without considering the faces of the people behind them? For him, it used to be all about the bottom line. He'd defined success in dollars, not in helping people.

"The article says you helped bail out a little shoe company that belongs to your date's family. Taking it under your wing, how heartwarming."

"That's what I'm good at." Building businesses, bringing them to success. Relationships, on the other hand, he completely sucked at.

"You're too modest, Nick. You're one of the best. I've never known you to let anything stand between you and success."

Truth was, it was Maddie who had bailed *him* out without his even knowing it. She'd awakened him to what was really important in life—looking at more than the bottom line. Taking time to enjoy people. Allowing yourself to love.

"It was a tiny company that's been around that small town for a lot of years."

"Small towns are fine to hail from, but for driven people like us, they don't lend much but weekend escape. Speaking of weekends, I'm heading off with a couple of friends to Vegas at the end of the month. Want to join me?"

Gayle gave him a hopeful look. Plates were being cleared. Soon dessert and coffee would be served, speakers would be introduced, awards given. The usual routine he'd repeated many, many times. Suddenly the room felt stifling. Nick loosened his tux tie. Checked his cell phone. No messages, not that there would be any from *her*.

Gayle was right. He rarely allowed anything to stand in the way of getting what he wanted. He had this time, all due to his big, pigheaded nature.

"Why are you taking your Rolex off?"

He barely heard the question. Something smacked him upside the head—maybe his own common sense, which had been gone far too long. All the holding back he'd done in his life had served him pretty well. Maybe losing your entire family in one fell swoop made a kid grow up guarded. Cutting people off when they got too close worked wonders for protecting your heart so nothing could ever hurt you like that again. Trouble was, he couldn't forget Maddie. She was too big, too wonderful, too *good*. He wanted to bask right in the middle of her circle of love and optimism.

His life of constantly pushing to acquire more and more businesses and money suddenly seemed meaningless. He didn't want that kind of life anymore. He wanted *her*.

Maybe it wasn't too late.

He turned to Gayle, then nodded politely to the rest of their table companions. "Something personal's come up. I'm sorry, but I've got to leave."

"Hope it's nothing serious." Gayle said.

"I left something in that small town I've got to retrieve."

Chapter Twenty-Two

Maddie looked down at her feet. She wore the prototype of the Bergdorf competition winning shoe, with lace and shining crystals and a silver platform that matched her sparkly silver dress. Samuel and she stood side by side on the stage, posing for picture after picture.

"How're your feet doing?" he asked.

"Tootsies are comfy as can be," she said, wiggling her toes, nails painted dark with silver sparkles to match the shoes. "Great engineering down there, Gramps."

"Excellent," he said.

The last time she'd been in front of a crowd, at the bachelor auction, she didn't have a clue what to do. Now she was made of stronger stuff. She smiled and proudly held the giant stiletto-shaped gold trophy they were presented. Kingston Shoes was coming back, and she was spearheading their resurrection, thanks to Samuel. They made a great creative team, and she'd learned so much from him in the past two months.

"This is getting heavy." She handed Samuel the golden shoe. "Here, you hold it for a while."

"Forget the trophy. I want the check," Samuel said.

"You sound like your grandson," Maddie said, then halted. *Oh, where did that come from?* She'd done so well today. She'd only looked around the spacious ballroom fifty odd times since they'd arrived. She'd only thought about Nick a thousand more.

Wouldn't he even show up for his own grandfather? They'd just won a national award. Orders were already pouring in for the brand they'd dubbed *Samuel Madison*. Upscale shoe stores were calling them, and the Buckleberry plant was gearing up production.

The photographers finally finished. Maddie linked arms with Samuel and steered him off the stage and down a set of stairs back to their table. Maddie's family flocked around, giving hugs and kisses.

"We're so proud of you, honey," Maddie's mom said. Her father stood and gave her a squeeze. Color was back in his face, and he was up to working half days now.

"Ditto," Derrick said. He and Jenna had flown in from Fort Bragg and were enjoying a weekend getaway without the twins.

Grandmeel, who stood a little off to the side, looked her usual elegant self in a classic black dress, pearls, and pumps. Maddie walked over to talk to her in private. "Congratulations," she said, as Maddie gave her a kiss on the cheek.

"Grandmeel, I want to apologize for my outburst in the boardroom this summer. I was harsh and hurtful. It was a bad time."

"Yes, you were rude. But I haven't been the best grandmother, have I?"

She looked hard at her grandmother, who must have been a real knockout in her time. Cat had definitely been the one to inherit her peaches-and-cream skin and delicate Southern beauty. "You're strong willed and tenacious, and I'd like to think I inherited some of that."

"Good qualities to survive attractions to Holter men," Grandmeel said.

"Maybe that attraction's not really over."

Maddie's heart stuttered on hearing the masculine voice. When she spun about, she found the wrong Holter. Samuel had approached her grandmother.

Amelia raised an elegant brow. "Men. They do get cocky when they win major awards, don't they?"

"Maybe so," Samuel said. "It's as good a time as any to invite you to dinner next week."

"*You* are inviting *me* to dinner?" Grandmeel said haughtily. "I'm seventy-two years old. I'm a great-grandmother, for God's sakes."

"You're still a beautiful woman, Amelia. Afterward, you could come over and watch the playoffs for the World Series on my big TV. What do you say?"

Maddie backed away to allow them some space and took a sip of her wine from the table. At least somebody was getting their happy ending tonight.

"Maybe Doris wasn't so crazy after all, about the happy endings, I mean."

The low tones of a familiar voice made Maddie whirl about for the second time. This time her heart full out stopped. Nick stood in front of her, looking movie-star gorgeous in an immaculate black tux and tie.

"I mean," he said, "not only did we get our families together, but everybody's working together again, too. I just need to change the end of that story."

"What story?"

Their gazes locked, and Maddie's heart skipped another beat. His eyes held a flicker of mischief.

Nick stepped closer. A five o'clock shadow outlined the strong lines of his jaw, and he looked a thousand times more handsome than in her daydreams. Except he looked a little tired, and he needed a haircut. Her whole body began trembling despite her resolve not to.

"I'm sorry I didn't tell you the truth about the shares. I knew it would piss you off. And you're right—I would have done anything to make it look like you succeeded, even if you didn't, and I know that was wrong. But I always believed in you, Maddie. I always knew you could do this."

He held out a plain white envelope.

She shook her head. "The company's going to be fine now. We don't need—"

"Open it," he said.

Maddie tore open the envelope and pulled out a single white sheet, typed and signed. A solitary dollar bill floated down and landed on the floor next to her heels.

Her eyes misted over and the words blurred. Barely able to speak, she called out to her father, who wheeled closer. She handed over the document, gesturing for him to read.

Her father put on his reading glasses and perused it. "It says he's allowed you to purchase all of his shares for the price of a dollar."

Maddie's heart wrenched. She forgot to breathe. Her

brain couldn't process. "You gave me all of your shares?"

"Well, technically he *sold* them to you," her dad said. "He's no longer the majority owner. *You* are."

Maddie bent to pick up the dollar. She traced the familiar old numbers scrawled with black Sharpie across the green background along with the words "Call Me."

She held a hand over her heart as a sharp, bittersweet ache filled her chest. It was the dollar she'd paid to Nick at the kissing booth so long ago.

"You kept it all these years."

"I told you, that was some kiss."

Nick had given everything back to her to do with as she wanted. Hell, he'd even given her dollar back.

"I know I've got a thing about control, but I don't want to control anything about your company, Maddie. I do believe in you, and I know you're responsible for your own success."

"You were right about me having to believe in myself. I think I've finally left my past behind me. You've made it possible. I never thanked you for all you've done. I'm glad you're here to see our first success."

"The first of many." He stepped forward and took up her hand. "I want to be around to see more of them too, if you'll let me."

Maddie dabbed at her eyes. Her mascara was running, but she couldn't stop crying. She felt lightheaded and flushed.

"So do you remember it—the story around the campfire?"

"I remember some stuff you made up about love and happily-ever-afters. Something about bringing everyone back together because that's what love does."

"That's what a *wedding* does."

The blood was really going to her head. Nick pulled her

close until they were face to face. His spicy cologne filled her nostrils.

Maddie was dizzy, the room was spinning. She could see her parents, Cat, Jenna and Derrick, Gramps and Grandmeel all standing there smiling. Then she looked into Nick's beautiful brown eyes, and they were full of tenderness and something much deeper she was afraid to name.

She didn't know exactly what he was going to say, but she sensed it was going to be good.

"I'll love you till the day I die. Now marry me."

"That's a little pushy, Holter," she finally managed to say. "I know you're used to bossing people around all day, but I'm going to need a little more than that."

"Okay." He took a deep breath and looked deep into her eyes. "I can only promise to love you forever, with all my heart and soul." He lowered himself to one knee. "*Please* marry me."

Oh, that was good. *Really* good.

Her eyes blurred, but in her peripheral vision she could see Cat bring her hands to her mouth in shock. Her mom gave a little clap and held onto her dad. Even Grandmeel threaded her arm through Samuel's.

Nick slipped something shiny and sparkly onto Maddie's finger, but she barely noticed. All she could see before her was the gorgeous, wonderful man she wanted to spend the rest of her life with. "Yes," she said. "I will."

He rose up and covered her lips softly with his, cupping her face in his strong hands and giving her a full-mouthed kiss that was slow and lush and perfect.

"I'm still dizzy," she said when it was through.

"Not too dizzy, I hope," he whispered in her ear. "The

evening is just beginning."

"Nicholas," his grandfather said. "It's about time you finally got your head out of your—"

Nick held up his hands. "Okay, okay, Gramps, I get it."

"One more thing." Samuel moved in menacingly close. "I never thanked you for giving me the chance I never thought I'd get. You're a good boy, Nicholas. I love you." His voice cracked on the last words.

Nick was never one to blush, but he was doing it now. If Maddie wasn't mistaken, his eyes were a little watery too. "Love you too, Gramps," he said in a low voice as they embraced.

"Join us for dinner, son," Henry said after a while, clapping Nick on the back. "We haven't had the chance to thank you for all you've done for us."

Rosalyn kissed him on both cheeks and hugged him. "More importantly, we want to welcome you to the family."

"I'd like that a lot." He glanced at his watch. "But we'll have to take a rain check. We're going on a little trip. If, of course, Maddie's agreeable."

"I don't have any clothes."

"Trust me, you won't be needing any."

Maddie blushed. "Nick! Our families are *right here*."

He reached behind him and pulled up a standard black wheelie bag. "I mean, you won't need any because I packed for you. OCD does have its uses."

Nick moved to kiss her again, but Grandmeel intervened. "You're not going to go gallivanting away with my granddaughter on some phony honeymoon without marrying her first. It's just not proper."

Samuel interrupted. "Amelia, for God's sakes, leave

them be. They've been apart long enough."

For once, Grandmeel said nothing.

"Don't you *dare* get married without me," Maddie's mom called out. "We want a service in the church. With flowers and bridesmaids and the whole family."

Maddie kissed her grandmother on the cheek. "It's all right, Grandmeel. Your objection's noted, but I'm still going."

Grandmeel shot a nasty glare at Derrick who pointed innocently at himself. "Don't look at me, 'Meel. I *like* the guy."

Madison kissed everyone and gave teary good-byes. She saved Cat for last.

"Cat, I'm so sorry about everything. I'll be able to pay you back now with the prize money from the competition."

Cat shrugged. "It's for the best, Maddie. Robert just wasn't The One. But I will take my money back. I always did want to see Hawaii."

Maddie hugged her sister hard. "You're the best sister ever."

"I know. And I'm fine." Cat brushed back her own tears and pushed Maddie away. "Now go have fun!"

Finally, Nick took Maddie's hand and led her out of the hotel.

"Where are we going, anyway?" Maddie asked, sneaking a peek at her beautiful sparkler, which she held out to catch the light at different angles.

Nick approached the curb and put his arm out to flag a cab. "Turns out I really do own a small Caribbean island."

"That's great, but Nick…" Maddie tugged on his arm until he stopped.

"Yes, Maddie?"

"Would it be okay to maybe get a room here tonight? I mean, it doesn't have to be anything big and fancy."

Nick frowned. "You really are afraid of flying. Unfortunately, we can't drive there."

"No, it's not that. It's just that we've wasted enough time, and I don't want to waste a second more. Not that I wouldn't love an oceanfront suite but right now the only view I want is your naked chest on top of me."

"Wow," Nick said. "I can't argue with that."

She kissed him impulsively on the cheek. "I still can't believe you saved that kissing booth dollar after all these years. There's only one problem."

Nick frowned. "What's that?"

"You were a shark even back then, because the dollar was meant to go to the Rescue Dogs' charity." She tapped him on the chest. "You weren't supposed to *keep* it."

Nick tossed back a laugh. "Kiss me again, and we can adopt one to make up for it."

She tugged on his sleeve. "Nick, one more thing." His eyes were dark and dangerous and lit with the same glow of happiness she felt inside. "I love you."

"I love you too, Madison. No more talking."

Then he kissed her again, and she knew it was the beginning of a whole lifetime of kisses.

About the Author

Miranda Liasson loves to write stories about courageous but flawed characters who find love despite themselves, because there's nothing like a great love story. And if there are a few laughs along the way, even better! She won the 2013 Romance Writers of America Golden Heart Award for Series Romance and also writes contemporary romance for Montlake Publishing. She lives in the Midwest with her husband, three kids, and office mates Maggie, a yellow lab, and Posey, a rescue cat with attitude. Miranda loves to hear from readers! Find her at mirandaliasson.com, Facebook. com/MirandaLiassonAuthor or on Twitter @mirandaliasson.

Printed in the USA
CPSIA information can be obtained
at www.ICGtesting.com
LVHW010259290524
781666LV00032B/805

9 781943 336517